and frightened. It whimpered, then lifted one tiny hand and pushed it through the bars. There was an ugly wound on the baby's wrist, edged with black scorch marks.

'It's been shot!' Jake gasped. He peered into the crate and saw that the baby wasn't alone. There were at least two others shut in there with it. And from what Jake could make out in the gloom, one of them looked in a very bad way. 'There's a really tiny one in here curled up in a heap,' he told Ross.

Ross looked grim. 'I'm going for help,' he said, 'You wait—'

Voices were coming their way, terrifyingly near. There was no chance to get out, or even hide.

We're done for, thought Jake, a shiver of fear running through him.

LUCY DANIELS

SAFARI SUMER HUNTED

Illustrated by
Pete Smith

*Hodder
Children's
Books*

a division of Hodder Headline Limi...

To Bean, who loves Africa too

Special thanks to Andrea Abbott

**Thanks also to everyone at the Born Free Foundation
(www.bornfree.org.uk) for reviewing the
wildlife information in this book**

Text copyright © 2003 Working Partners Limited
Created by Working Partners Limited, London W6 0QT
Illustration copyright © 2003 Pete Smith

First published in Great Britain in 2003
by Hodder Children's Books

The rights of Lucy Daniels and Pete Smith to be identified
as the Author and Illustrator respectively of the Work
have been asserted by them in accordance with the
Copyright, Designs and Patents Act 1988.

For more information about Lucy Daniels,
please visit www.animalark.co.uk

10 9 8 7 6 5 4 3 2 1

A Catalogue record for this book is available from
the British Library

ISBN 0 340 85123 6

Typeset in Palatino by Avon DataSet Ltd,
Bidford-on-Avon, Warwickshire

Printed and bound in Great Britain by
Clays Ltd, St Ives plc

The paper and board used in this paperback by
Hodder Children's Books are natural recyclable products
made from wood grown in sustainable forests.
The manufacturing processes conform to the environmental
regulations of the country of origin.

Hodder Children's Books
a division of Hodder Headline Limited
338 Euston Road
London NW1 3BH

ONE

A shaft of sunlight fell on Jake Berman's face, waking him up. He opened his eyes and felt puzzled for a second. There was no ceiling above him – just endless blue sky. Then the steady thrumming of an engine reminded him where he was – on board a ferry crossing Lake Victoria from Tanzania to Uganda in East Africa.

Feeling hot inside his sleeping bag, Jake wriggled out of it. He sat up and glanced around at the other passengers sprawled out on the top deck of MV *Victoria*. Most of them were still asleep, but a few were beginning to stir. Near the stern, a woman was cooking a pan of eggs on a small portable gas stove. A sleepy-eyed toddler clung to her skirt, sucking his thumb.

Jake stretched and yawned, then fell into a fit of coughing as something caught in his throat.

Next to him, his mum, Hannah, rolled over in her

sleeping bag. 'Swallowed a fly?' she asked him, drowsily.

'Yes,' Jake wheezed between coughs. He fished around in his backpack for a bottle of water. Finding it, he pulled off the lid and glugged down thirsty mouthfuls until the bottle was empty. Water had never tasted so good!

'Yuck! That was disgusting!' he grimaced, still feeling an unpleasant stickiness at the back of his throat. 'I thought we'd left those flies behind.'

During the night, they'd passed through a swarm of the notorious lake flies that hatched in their millions at full moon. Everyone on the deck had dived for cover under sleeping bags, blankets and mosquito nets to avoid breathing in the insects. Jake had even found himself wishing they'd spent the night in a cabin instead of out in the open. But it had been his idea to sleep on deck, so he had no one to blame but himself.

Hannah pushed back her sleeping bag and rubbed her eyes. 'I don't think it's possible to escape water flies,' she said. 'The Great Lakes region is full of them. Look, there's a swarm now.' She pointed to a huge brown cloud hovering above the water to the south of them.

'It looks like smoke,' Jake remarked, relieved the ferry was going in the opposite direction. He rolled up his sleeping bag and strapped it to the bottom of his rucksack, then went to lean over the railings to see if he could spot land. But all he could see was an unbroken expanse of shimmering water.

Jake hadn't expected Lake Victoria to be so enormous, even though his stepdad, Rick, had told him it was about the size of Ireland. But soon after the ferry sailed out of the port of Mwanza in northern Tanzania yesterday afternoon, Jake saw for himself just how vast the lake was. Very quickly, the land slipped over the horizon and as far as the eye could see, there was nothing but water. It was like being on the open sea, except the waves were smaller and there was no salt in the air.

Jake looked at his watch. Nearly seven o'clock – still at least an hour to go before they docked at Port Bell in Uganda. He drummed impatiently on the metal railings. They'd been on the boat for about nineteen hours, he calculated. It had been great at first, especially last night when they'd stretched out on the deck under the huge white moon. Until, of course, the flies arrived.

But the flies weren't the real reason Jake couldn't wait to get off the MV *Victoria*. As soon as they docked in Uganda, he and his mum were heading west to a conservation centre called Luama. For the very first time, Jake was going to see chimpanzees in the wild. Since coming to live in Tanzania a few months ago, he had seen more wildlife than he could have dreamed of. Just about every day he came face to face with monkeys and baboons, but so far he hadn't seen any of the Great Apes that lived in Africa – the chimpanzees and gorillas that lived under constant threat of extinction in the dense equatorial forests.

'Can you see land yet?' asked Hannah, coming to stand next to him.

Jake shook his head. 'Not yet.'

'That means we have time for breakfast,' said his mum. She reached into her backpack, took out a bunch of bananas and handed one to Jake.

'What do you think I am? A chimp?' Jake laughed, taking the banana and peeling it.

'Well, we *are* their closest relative,' his mother teased.

'I know. Rick told me that their DNA is almost the same as ours,' Jake said.

Hannah finished her banana then pushed her rucksack close to Jake's. 'Keep an eye on my things while I go and wash,' she told him.

Jake sat down next to the two backpacks and the big aluminium case that held Hannah's expensive camera and lenses. His mum was a freelance wildlife photographer and journalist, and it was because of this they were on their way to Luama. Hannah's latest project was an article on chimp behaviour for an international wildlife magazine. She'd heard about Luama through friends of Rick's, and had contacted the wardens, Liz and David Kirby. The Kirbys had immediately invited the Bermans to spend a week with them.

Pity Rick couldn't come with us, thought Jake, crossing his long legs and leaning against his backpack. But Rick hadn't been able to leave Musabi, the Tanzanian game reserve he managed, because his right-hand man, Morgan Rafiki, was in hospital recovering from a serious bout of malaria. *At least Bina won't be lonely*, Jake thought, picturing the tiny orphaned dik-dik he had hand-reared. Bina's mother had been taken by an eagle so the Bermans had adopted the baby antelope. Jake and his friend, Shani, who was Morgan's niece, had bottle-fed Bina for several weeks. But now that the tiny animal was weaned, she roamed about freely in the big garden surrounding the Bermans' house at the edge of Musabi.

When Hannah came back, Jake pulled a change of clothing out of his rucksack and made his way through the crowds to the men's room. By the time he joined his mother again, the Ugandan mainland was clearly visible, a dark green band on the horizon.

'It looks like it's all jungle there,' Jake commented, scanning the irregular coastline through his binoculars. Thick tropical vegetation grew right up to the water's edge. It looked so dense that Jake wondered how people actually reached the lake.

The ferry cruised steadily towards the shore and soon Jake could see small mud shacks hugging the water's edge. After a while, the wooden huts gave way to big white colonial houses, and when Jake saw a building that was signposted *Bell Beer Brewery*, he knew they'd arrived at Port Bell.

With a juddering bump, the *Victoria* came to a stop against the harbour wall. The passengers surged to the exits, pushing and jostling as they waited for the crew to let down the gangplanks.

'Let's go,' said Hannah, heaving her rucksack on to her shoulders and picking up her camera case as a deckhand opened the gate nearest them.

Jake followed his mum down the bouncing wooden gangplank. They joined the throngs waiting to go through passport control, where an official studied their British passports and visas for what seemed like ages. Finally, he waved them through, wishing them a pleasant holiday in his country.

'David Kirby said we'd spot him easily,' said Hannah as they went out into the street.

'You sure?' Jake asked. He looked around doubtfully, his green eyes squinting against the unforgiving tropical sun.

Minibus taxis blocked the narrow street, hooting loudly. A bicycle carrying three people wobbled wildly between the taxis, then took a short cut by mounting the pavement, narrowly missing several pedestrians who ducked out of the way at the last moment.

'How does anyone find anyone else here?' Jake muttered, jumping out of the way of another bicycle that was careening towards him.

'Quite easily, it seems,' smiled Hannah as a broad-shouldered, dark-haired man suddenly appeared from behind a taxi and came over to them. On the front of his bright yellow T-shirt was a picture of a chimpanzee's face. 'That's got to be David,' Hannah laughed.

'Hannah and Jake Berman, I presume,' said the man when he reached them. 'I'm David Kirby. It's great to meet you at last. We've really been looking forward to your visit.'

'So have we,' Jake said enthusiastically. 'I can't wait to see the chimps.'

Hannah frowned at him and Jake suddenly realized how rude he must have sounded. 'Er, sorry,' he said quickly. 'It's just that . . .'

David's friendly brown eyes danced with amusement. 'I know what you mean,' he said. 'And I agree with you. Chimps are fascinating – much more so than dull humans.' He took Hannah's rucksack from her and swung it over his shoulder. 'Even though I've been studying them for ten years, I'm still mesmerized by them. And you will be too. You won't have to wait long – we'll be going out at first light tomorrow to look for your first community.' He led Jake and Hannah across the road and up a narrow alley to another street where Jake spotted a green jeep double-parked next to a van.

'That's us,' said David, pointing to the mud-spattered vehicle. 'The only parking place I could find.' Through the grime that coated the front door of the jeep, Jake could just make out the Luama logo – the same chimp face as the one on David's T-shirt.

The jeep's windows were also speckled with mud so it wasn't until they'd reached the vehicle that Jake noticed someone a few years older than himself sitting behind the steering wheel. He had thick dark hair and looked a lot like David. Jake realized at once that this must be Ross, the Kirbys' fifteen-year-old son.

'No problems, Ross?' asked David, confirming Jake's guess as he opened the back door and put Hannah's backpack inside.

'No,' said Ross, sliding out of the driver's seat on to the pavement and giving his dad the car keys. He glanced sideways at Jake and winked. 'I was kind of hoping the van driver would come back so I'd have to move out of his way. I could do with some driving practice.'

'A good thing it didn't happen,' said David, nodding towards a serious-faced policeman who was coming towards them. 'Let's get out of here quickly.' He opened the front passenger door for Hannah then hurried round to the driver's side while Jake and Ross climbed into the back.

David started the engine and pulled away, leaving a bemused-looking policeman staring after them.

Ross wound down his window then turned to Jake. 'Have a nice trip?'

'Yes and no,' Jake answered, also opening his window and leaning forward into the cooling breeze.

'Don't tell me! Lake flies,' chuckled Ross.

'You've got it,' Jake laughed.

They left the town and headed west along a bumpy pot-holed road. After a few kilometres, the jeep was the only vehicle in sight, and instead of the buildings of Port Bell, there was now just thick vegetation on either side of the road. Eventually, the tar petered out and the road worsened, making driving difficult. They made very slow progress as David steered carefully past deep puddles and long stretches of churned-up mud. Jake could understand why the jeep was so dirty!

'Believe it or not, it's often worse than this,' said David, engaging first gear and coaxing the jeep up a bumpy slope.

'Specially in April,' put in Ross, 'when it rains really heavily. Then the road turns to soup!'

'Hey! Look at that!' Jake burst out as they rounded a bend. Just ahead, bang in the middle of the road, stood the remains of a bombed-out tank. 'Where did that come from?'

'It's left over from the war some years ago,' said David, slowing down to drive round the rusting hulk.

'War!' Jake echoed, staring out of his window at the cannon that was pointing straight at him. Straggly weeds grew up the sides of the sand-coloured tank, and a lanky tree sprouted from the turret. 'Who was fighting?' he asked.

'Tanzania and Uganda,' Hannah told him.

Jake was surprised, and oddly uncomfortable, to think that the country he now regarded as home had been at war with Uganda. 'What was it about?' he asked.

'It was all very complicated,' said David. 'But the main thing is that things are peaceful now.' A mongoose scurried down a bank at the side of the road and dived under the tank.

'At least some good came out of the fighting,' said Ross, pointing to the mongoose that was peeping out at them from his burnt-out hideaway.

'Mmm. But animals really suffered during it,' said David soberly. 'Chimps and gorillas had an especially hard time. Unfortunately, things are still tough for them today, mainly because of all the logging. It's shrinking their habitat, and making it way too easy for poachers to target them.'

'That's why places like Luama are so important,' added Ross.

'Have you rescued lots of chimps?' Jake asked, taking a last glance out of the back window at the ugly reminder of the war.

'Dozens,' Ross answered.

'Most of them from the illegal pet trade,' said David.

Jake winced. Not long ago, he wouldn't have seen much wrong with keeping a chimp as a pet, as long as it was well looked after. But since he'd come to Africa, he'd learned to look at wildlife in a new way – a way that understood the wildness in animals and their right to live a natural life where they belonged. This had really been brought home to him a few months ago when he'd been involved in reuniting a pair of lion cubs with their mother, then releasing them into the wild.

They drove on through tumbledown villages where giggling children waved shyly from the doors of grass huts. If Jake and Ross waved back, the delighted boys and girls charged out on to the road and ran behind the jeep until they grew tired and stopped, grinning and waving until they disappeared from view.

Leaving the villages behind, the dusty road took them past huge cleared areas dotted with blackened tree stumps. 'Not long ago these were magnificent tropical forests,' David explained. He slowed down so that they could have a good look at one particularly vast and muddy clearing. Apart from a lone brown bird flitting from stump to stump, nothing moved.

'It's like a wasteland,' Jake remarked.

'That's just what it is,' agreed David. 'And that's all that's left of the forest,' he added, pointing to a huge pile of logs being loaded on to the back of a flat-bed truck on the far side of the barren land.

He accelerated again, and within a few kilometres the desolate acres were just a speck in the background while tangled vegetation grew thickly at the sides of the road.

'I had no idea Luama was such a long way from Port Bell,' said Hannah, staring out at the dense tropical bush. 'You must have left home in the middle of the night to come and fetch us, David.'

'Not really,' David replied. 'We're usually up at the crack of dawn anyway. And,' he added, winking at Ross in his rear view mirror, 'we didn't exactly amble along, did we?'

'You can say that again,' said Ross. He grinned at Jake. 'Dad fancies himself as a rally driver.'

'And what about you?' David retorted. 'You're not a sedate driver yourself.'

Jake looked at Ross with admiration. 'Can you really drive?' he asked.

'Sort of,' said Ross. 'Dad lets me practise on the track to Luama.' He leaned out of his window. 'That's it there.'

Just ahead, a faded sign pointed to the right. David shifted gear and turned off the road on to a narrow track that meandered through towering trees with silvery trunks and pale green leaves. Jake kept his eyes peeled, expecting to see a chimpanzee at any moment. But the only primates he saw were some baboons crashing their way through the forest ahead of them, their dark brown shapes blending easily with their surroundings.

Jake couldn't help feeling surprised when they finally pulled up at the research centre. He hadn't known quite what to expect, maybe a few wooden buildings and a log house for the Kirbys. He certainly hadn't imagined that Luama would be just like an overgrown camp site. There were a number of green tents standing on raised wooden platforms. The front fly sheets were extended like roofs so that each tent had its own veranda that overlooked a small lake a few hundred metres away.

Marshy wetland lay between the tents and the lake, while beyond the blue water a dark green jungle rose steeply up the slopes of a mountain. Climbing out of the jeep, Jake could see flocks of herons and rather ugly marabou storks standing silently amongst the reeds near the lake, their heads on one side as they stared at the water. They looked as if they were listening for fish moving about in the shallows.

Jake glanced round the encampment. Apart from the tents, the only other man-made structures were a small wooden building and a few thatched shelters in a fenced-off area to one side.

'What's the enclosure for?' Jake asked Ross as they took the backpacks out of the jeep.

'It's a holding pen, in case we need to keep chimps under observation, or wait for them to be released,'

Ross explained. He walked towards the tents. 'Come on. I'll show you round.'

In the middle of the camp a tall reed fence encircled an area where canvas chairs stood round a rock-lined hearth in the ground.

'That's the boma, where we have our meals when it's not raining,' Ross continued.

'And when it rains?' Jake asked.

'We eat in the lounge,' Ross said, pointing to a big tent in front of them.

Just then, a fair-haired woman who was about a head shorter than Ross came out on to the wooden deck of the lounge. 'Hi there,' she said, looking first at Jake then at Hannah who was just behind him. 'I'm Liz Kirby. It's fantastic to see you.' She leaned on the wooden railing and smiled at David who was walking next to Hannah. 'We don't get a lot of visitors out here, do we?'

'What do you mean?' laughed David. 'Our relatives are always dropping by.'

'You mean, the chimps come into camp?' Jake asked, guessing what David meant by 'relatives'.

'Not too often,' said Liz. 'We try not to encourage them, because we don't want them depending on us for anything.'

'Other than their safety,' put in David, 'and even that we can't guarantee.'

'Still, we do our best,' said Liz cheerfully. She looked at Ross. 'Show Hannah and Jake where their tents are so that they can unpack and freshen up. When everyone's ready we'll meet for lunch in the boma.'

Jake's tent was close to the holding pen. From his veranda he had an unobstructed view of the wooden shelters. *Pity there aren't any chimps in there now*, he thought. Still, it was going to be even better when he saw them in their natural forest habitat tomorrow. Jake could hardly wait. He dumped his backpack on the old tin trunk that served as a bedside table, then stretched out on the bed, intending to close his eyes for just a few minutes. After his restless night on the ferry, he was suddenly feeling rather worn out.

He awoke to find the daylight almost gone. *I must have been asleep for hours*, he thought, feeling a bit cross with himself for dropping off like that. He sat up and splashed some water on his face from a jug next to his bed, then he went out on to the veranda and looked across to the lake that glistened in the fading sun.

From the forest came the piercing calls of birds, and Jake's keen eyes spotted an eagle flying low over the water. It was an African fish eagle, searching for a last meal before the sun went down.

Jake listened hard, trying not to focus on the croaking of frogs in the marsh and the shrill chorus of crickets that were waking up with the dying of the day. What he really wanted to hear was chimpanzees. Yet he wasn't quite sure what to expect. He knew chimps made a high-pitched shrieking noise, but was that all? And would they be so noisy in the forest? Or would they move about silently to avoid being seen?

He started down the steps of his veranda but was stopped in his tracks as a series of loud bangs echoed from the forest. Gunfire! Another volley of shots rang out and Jake saw dozens of birds flapping out from the trees. He stood frozen to the spot as there came another round of shooting and then, finally, silence.

An empty, heavy silence that filled Jake with dread.

TWO

Jake leaped down the last few steps and charged across the camp to the boma. Halfway there, he met Ross running in the same direction.

'What is it?' Jake panted.

'Poachers, I think,' Ross said grimly as they dashed into the boma where Hannah and the Kirbys were sitting around the unlit fire. The three adults looked equally stern-faced. Their drinks stood untouched on a folding wooden table in front of them, and they were leaning forward, talking earnestly.

'It's probably the same gang that attacked that community in July,' David was saying to Liz.

'What community? I thought you said the war was over,' Jake said.

Liz looked at him, her eyes full of sadness. 'Those guns weren't being fired at people, Jake. We think this is a gang of poachers that ambushed a community of chimps in the south of the reserve. They were killed for their meat.'

Jake stared at her. 'Killed for their meat?' he echoed. 'But people don't eat chimps!'

'Actually, a lot of people do,' said David. 'Chimps have been on the bushmeat menu in Africa for thousands of years.'

'But aren't the chimps protected?' Jake protested.

'They're supposed to be,' answered Ross. 'But that doesn't mean much to the commercial bushmeat hunters. Chimp meat fetches a good price, both in the towns and overseas.' He picked up a long stick and started poking at the logs in the fireplace. A leggy spider scrambled out from beneath the kindling and scurried up the stick towards Ross's hand. He flicked it off and it disappeared under the rocks surrounding the hearth.

'The trouble is, professional hunters are experts at covering their tracks,' David explained. 'That's why they attack just before nightfall like this, because they know we can't track them in the dark.'

Jake slumped down in a chair and stared at the ground. 'I wish we could do something,' he muttered.

David reached for his beer but instead of drinking it, he held it in one hand. 'All we can do is wait for first light, then see if we can find where the attack happened,' he said. He studied the liquid in his glass for a while then took a sip and put it down again. 'With any luck, the hunters may have left some evidence behind. We'll catch them one day, I'm sure.'

It was still dark and drizzling steadily when the search party gathered in the lounge tent the next morning. There were six of them: Jake and Hannah, Ross and David, and two scouts, Richard Syandira and Nkonko Gamalu, who had worked at Luama for many years. They came from a nearby village so they knew the area well. They were also very skilled at tracking the chimpanzees in the dense forest.

Jake had spent a fitful night mulling over what he'd learned about the cruel and sordid bushmeat trade. Nevertheless, he couldn't help feeling excited this morning at the prospect of finding chimpanzees living in the wild. He guessed they'd be very wary of humans, especially after last night's attack. *So we might only get a glimpse of them*, he thought to himself as he slung a small knapsack containing a packed lunch and two bottles of water over his shoulders.

'Take care,' Liz called after them. She was staying behind in radio contact with the group, in case there was trouble and they needed to call the police.

Jake looked at the radio sticking out of Ross's shirt

pocket. 'Do you think things will turn nasty?' he asked him in a low voice.

Ross stooped down to tie up a loose bootlace. 'Probably not.' He straightened up again and shrugged his shoulders to position his backpack more comfortably. 'The poachers will be miles away by now. We'll be lucky to find their footprints.'

With Nkonko and David in front and Richard at the back, the group followed a well-worn path leading out of the camp. Day was just breaking as they entered the forest, but it was so dark and gloomy under the trees that Jake couldn't see much ahead of him.

The drizzle soon turned to light rain. Trickles of cold water dripped down the back of Jake's neck and seeped into his clothes. He pulled up the hood of his anorak and tied the string tightly under his neck. But the rain dripped off the hood and on to his face, then ran down his neck into his shirt. 'I hope this doesn't go on all day,' he muttered.

'What did you say?' asked Ross, half-turning to hear Jake more clearly.

'The rain,' said Jake. 'I hope it stops.'

'It probably won't,' said Ross, grinning as he pulled his jacket closer round himself. 'Not at this time of the year.'

Jake groaned. He was beginning to feel a bit

disillusioned with the whole chimp expedition. Why had his mum brought them here in the rainy season? He looked over his shoulder at Hannah who was a little way behind him. She had stopped and was tucking her camera inside her raincoat to keep it dry.

'But it's the best time to come to the forest,' Ross went on as if he could read Jake's thoughts. He wiped a sodden strand of his jet-black hair off his forehead. 'If you want to see chimps termiting, that is.'

'What's that?' Jake asked, suddenly feeling interested again in spite of the rain.

Without stopping, Ross plucked a long grass stalk growing next to the path. He reached back and handed it to Jake like a relay baton. 'It's when chimps put a grass stick like this in ant holes to catch termites.'

'Why do they do that?' Jake frowned, quickening his pace to keep up with Ross. Jake was tall for a thirteen-year-old, but his long stride couldn't match that of Ross who was already almost as tall as his dad.

'To eat,' said Ross. 'They love termites.'

Jake was surprised. 'As much as bananas?' he asked.

'Dunno,' laughed Ross. 'You'd have to ask a chimp that.'

'I will when I meet one.' Jake grinned. Then, more seriously, he asked, 'Will we definitely find chimps?'

Ross shrugged. 'Who knows? Sometimes when we track them we come across one or two communities, and other times we don't even hear them. I guess it's just luck really. But Richard and Nkonko are brilliant at finding them. They even know how to call them.'

'Really? Do the chimps answer?' Jake asked.

'Sometimes,' said Ross.

'I hope they do this time,' Jake said quietly, looking round.

The forest here was dense enough to block out the soft light of dawn. Jake peered up into the towering tree canopy. Through the dark foliage, he could see patches of grey sky. 'Not very promising,' he muttered to himself, wiping the rain off his face with the back of his hand.

It was eerily silent. Apart from the group's soft footfalls on the soggy ground, the occasional snapping of a fallen branch when it was stepped on, and the *drip-drip-drip* of rain on leaves, Jake could hear only a few birdcalls high up in the trees. But as the sky grew lighter the chorus increased and, after about an hour, the forest became filled with echoing birdsong.

'There must be millions of birds in here,' Jake said to Ross.

'I guess so,' said Ross. 'But I don't know a lot about them. You'd have to ask my mum. She's the bird expert in the family.'

The path petered out and disappeared. Jake wondered how the scouts knew which way to go. There seemed to be no landmarks, just thick tangled vegetation all around. Lianas dangled from the trees and Jake could imagine chimpanzees swinging from them. He grabbed one of the thick twining plants, but he hadn't spotted the sharp spines growing from it. 'Ouch!' he said, feeling a thorn pierce the palm of his hand. He rolled his hand into a fist to staunch the blood.

'That wasn't very smart,' said Hannah, offering him a tissue.

'I know.' Jake shrugged, feeling a bit embarrassed as he dabbed at the hole the thorn had made. 'I thought they were like ropes. The chimps must have tough hands!'

'Ssh,' whispered Richard suddenly, his finger to his lips and his eyes wide with expectation.

Jake froze. Had the scout heard a chimpanzee? Rooted to the spot, they waited silently. Just as Jake began to think Richard hadn't heard anything unusual, a brown blur flashed past them and went leaping away into the forest on long athletic legs.

'What was that?' Jake asked, blinking in surprise.

'Bushbuck,' said Richard. 'He got a bigger fright than we did!'

They continued in silence up a steep slope. The thick leaf mould beneath them was very slippery from the rain and Jake had to grab on to tree branches to stop himself from sliding down the hill. Climbing alongside Jake, Ross lost his footing altogether and, unable to grab a branch in time, landed heavily on the ground then slid several metres downhill until a moss-covered tree stump broke his fall.

'Oh, great!' he said, picking himself up and shaking off the damp leaves clinging to his clothes.

'Are you OK?' Hannah called down to him.

'Yeah. Nothing broken,' said Ross, hauling himself back up the slope.

A solid wall of undergrowth confronted them further up the hill. To Jake, it looked impenetrable. But Nkonko and David began pushing their way through it.

'They've got to be kidding,' said Hannah, crouching down to watch the two men crawl through a narrow gap.

'It's not too bad,' Jake said over his shoulder as he dropped to his knees and followed them, leopard-crawling on his stomach and keeping his head tucked in to protect his eyes from thorns and sticks.

'Not too bad!' repeated Hannah behind him. 'Yeah, right. As long as you're a teenager or an ex-marine!'

There was a small glade on the other side of the thicket. 'Let's have a rest here,' said David, helping Hannah to her feet as she emerged from the bushes. 'Sorry about that,' he added. 'But we didn't have much choice there.'

Hannah shrugged and clapped the mud off her hands. 'I've experienced worse,' she said. 'Rick's never been afraid to show me the grubbier side of trekking!' She lifted her camera and focussed it on the soggy-looking group. 'Smile, everyone,' she said. She caught Jake's eye and winked. 'Or grimace, if you prefer.'

The shutter clicked, almost masking another noise that came from somewhere deeper in the forest, a muffled, low-pitched grunting sound. Jake knew instinctively it was a sound they'd all been waiting to hear.

'Chimpanzee,' whispered Richard.

Jake shivered with excitement as the grunt came again, this time much louder. 'Are they close?' he whispered to David.

'It's hard to tell,' answered David quietly. 'Their calls can travel for miles.'

Nkonko crept to the edge of the glade and listened. The grunting came again. Nkonko waited a few moments then cupped his hands around his mouth and called out. *'Hoo!'*

Jake held his breath, waiting to hear a chimp reply. Nothing.

Nkonko repeated the call. *'Hoo, hoo, hoo.'* The low-pitched sounds echoed through the trees. *'Hoo, hoo,'* the scout called again, finishing with a drawn-out breathy, *'waaa.'*

They must have heard that, Jake thought. He listened intently, trying to ignore the bird calls and the rhythmic *drip, drip, drip* of the rain. And suddenly, there it was again – a distinctive grunt, more high-pitched than before. After a brief pause, there came another sound, almost identical to the call Nkonko had made. *Hoo, hoo, hoo, waaaa.*

Jake could hardly believe it. The chimps were answering back! They must be OK then, despite last night's gunfire. 'Do you think these chimps could be the ones the hunters attacked yesterday?' he whispered to Ross.

'Could be,' said Ross in a low voice. 'Just because some are answering doesn't mean the whole community is safe. The poachers might have shot one or two of them for meat. But we'll only be able to tell when we see them.'

'How?' Jake asked.

'Dad and the scouts know most of the

communities,' whispered Ross. 'So they'll know if anyone's missing. Also the chimps might be very nervous, much more than usual.'

David beckoned to the group. 'Let's go,' he said softly.

They started out from the glade and were clambering over an enormous fallen tree trunk when Jake heard a disturbance in the trees above them. He looked up, right into the face of a large white and red monkey.

Jake nudged Ross and pointed to the handsome animal. 'What kind of monkey's that?'

'Red colobus,' said Ross, and no sooner had he spoken than the forest canopy suddenly became alive as more of the monkeys appeared, swinging easily through the trees, their long, thick tails helping them balance. Jake estimated there must have been at least fifty of them. 'Looks like they're in a big hurry,' he said, watching the primates leap from tree to tree.

'They must have heard the chimps too,' said David.

'So what? Why the hurry?' Jake frowned.

Hannah touched his arm. 'They don't want to be the chimps' next meal,' she said quietly.

Jake looked at her aghast. 'Chimps eat monkeys?'

Ross nodded. 'And baboons, and bushbuck and bushpigs.'

'You're kidding!' exclaimed Jake, his mental image of gentle, fruit-eating chimpanzees suddenly taking on a different colour.

'Chimps aren't the peace-loving vegetarians we like to think they are,' put in David. 'In fact, they're pretty ferocious hunters. But I'll spare you the gory details. It could put you off chimps for life!' He swatted a mosquito that had landed on his neck.

Jake was intrigued, but he decided he'd rather not find out any more right now. He'd just settle for knowing that chimpanzees were meat eaters.

They pressed on, Richard and Nkonko taking turns to call out to the chimps. Every now and then there came a reply, and each time it was louder. After a while, Nkonko stopped and whispered almost inaudibly, 'We're very close now.'

Jake felt his heart lurch. Any moment now, he'd see his first wild chimpanzee!

Nkonko crept forward, beckoning the others to follow. Jake walked as lightly as he could, more conscious than ever of every snapping twig and dull footfall. He became aware of a low grunting, and then another and another. The chimpanzees must be only metres away! Next to Jake, Hannah removed the cover from her camera lens. She glanced at him and he saw that his mum was as excited as he was, her eyes shining.

Jake stared hard into the thickets ahead, then up into the tree canopy. The sky was a lot lighter now, improving the visibility in the forest. Jake wondered if the chimps would be up in the trees. Or on the forest floor? He peered ahead into the dense bushes again. A ray of sun penetrated the canopy. And in that beam, for the briefest moment, a dark shadowy shape appeared. In the blink of an eye, it vanished, but Jake was sure it had been a chimpanzee.

THREE

'Over there. Past those bushes,' whispered Nkonko.

Cautiously Jake crept behind Nkonko and David towards where the bulky shadow had been. The others moved stealthily behind him. They edged their way round a thick bush then came to an abrupt halt. About fifty metres ahead was a group of chimpanzees feeding on fruit that had fallen from a spreading fig tree.

'Wow!' Jake breathed, crouching down next to Ross. It was the most brilliant sight! Sitting on their haunches, the chimpanzees were peacefully sorting through the figs, looking for the juiciest ones.

'It's the B-group,' whispered David. To Jake's relief he added, 'I don't think they were the target last night.'

Jake was amazed that David could identify the chimpanzees so quickly. He made a mental note to ask him how he could tell them apart from other groups.

'I agree. They're not edgy at all,' observed Nkonko quietly.

Jake watched one of the chimps, a huge, serious-faced individual, snap off the stalk from a fig with its nimble, hairless fingers, then break open the fruit to inspect it closely before popping it into its mouth.

'That's Babu,' whispered Ross, following Jake's gaze. 'His name means "grandfather". He's one of the oldest chimps in this community.'

Another chimp loped over to a smaller one that was lying on the ground. 'Who are those two?' Jake asked Ross quietly.

'I'm not sure,' said Ross. 'The big one's a male – they're always a lot bigger than the females. And I think the little one's a girl called Bandia.'

Next to them, Richard nodded. 'Yes. The small one's Bandia and the male is Banja,' he whispered.

Banja began parting Bandia's thick black fur with his hands, looking for parasites. A second chimp, another male about the same size as Banja, came over and joined in the grooming session. Meanwhile Bandia lay very still, an utterly human expression of contentment on her pinky-brown face.

Jake did a quick count. Eight chimps, ranging in size from a small baby clinging to its mother's belly to the enormous Babu, who was much bigger than Jake had imagined chimps would grow.

Standing upright, the old chimp was about as tall as an average-sized man. And with the powerful muscles rippling in his chest and arms, he looked a lot stronger than most men!

Jake watched in amazement as a mother chimp, whose left ear was torn and misshapen, picked up a fig and offered it to her baby.

'That's Bibi and her baby boy, Buu,' said David.

Jake knew that Bibi was the Swahili word for lady and he seemed to remember that Buu meant grub!

Buu took the fig, sniffed it, then stuffed it into his mouth before slipping out of his mother's arms. With his cheeks bulging, he ran over to play with another infant.

A movement in a nearby tree made Jake look up. Three more chimps were clambering about in the branches. *That makes eleven*, Jake told himself. Eleven chimpanzees all in one place, and all of them seemingly oblivious to their human audience.

Suddenly Bibi, the torn-eared mother chimp, looked up and stared straight at Jake with eyes that were incredibly human. Intelligent, dark brown eyes that flashed with anger and suspicion!

Jake froze, not daring to breathe.

Bibi studied him for a moment, her brown-black hair puffed out menacingly and her lips pressed tightly together. She made a noise that sounded like a nervous cough. The rest of the community immediately stopped what they were doing and looked around, some of them uttering the same coughing bark.

Bibi stood upright. Even though she was at least a head or two shorter than the old male, she looked very powerful. She opened her mouth wide and barked, *Waa!* before taking a step forward and yelling menacingly, *Wraaa!*

Immediately some of the others echoed the call. *Wraaa*, they shrieked, standing on their hind legs, while the younger ones took cover behind the adults.

Jake was terrified. He was sure the big female was threatening him. Out of the corner of his eye, he noticed his mum shrink back as the chimpanzee took a step towards them, barking out another blood-curdling, *Waa!*

Just then, Richard crept forward into the clearing. 'It's OK. It's OK, Bibi,' he said calmly. 'It's me. Richard. Your friend. You know me. *Hoo, hoo, waa,'* he panted softly. He sat down, drew his knees up to his chest and, not looking at Bibi, pant-hooted quietly again while pretending to scratch in the ground for fruit.

Bibi relaxed at once. Dropping on to all fours, she ambled across to the scout, her lips stretched into a grin. When she was a few metres from him, she sat down, picked up a fig, put it in her mouth and chewed it with a satisfied smile on her dark, wrinkled face.

Jake felt giddy with relief. What amazing creatures they were! So gentle and affectionate one moment, ferocious and fearless the next. But if they were really fierce, how could the hunters get them so easily? *Probably because they're no match for a gun*, Jake reasoned, watching Bibi shuffling across to sit right next to Richard.

Seeing Bibi calm, the rest of the community settled down again.

Bibi ate another fig then stood up and, leaning forward on the knuckles of her hands, loped across to her little son and his friend who were tumbling together at the base of the tree.

Jake laughed quietly as Bibi's baby scrambled on to her back and clung on tightly, looking for all the world like a tiny jockey! Bibi pant-hooted again then strolled into the forest. Within moments she was out of sight.

Slowly, the rest of the group followed Bibi. The last to leave was a young male who couldn't resist one last look at Richard. Grunting softly, he strolled over to the scout and began prodding him with his leathery black hand.

'No! You find your own fruit, Baya,' chuckled Richard, trying to push the chimp away. But Baya persisted and before Richard could stand up, the chimpanzee had fished a banana out of his pocket.

'No,' Richard repeated, trying to cling to the banana. But the persistent ape simply jerked the banana out of Richard's grasp then ran away on his hind legs, rocking from side to side and peeling his prize as he went.

Jake laughed. 'What does Baya mean?' he asked Ross.

'Naughty,' came the reply.

'That figures!' Jake grinned. 'Did you take a picture of that, Mum?'

'Several,' said Hannah. She looked at David. 'So this community wasn't the target of the poachers last night?'

'No,' said David, standing up and stamping some ants off his boots. 'This is a particularly stable group, and I could see immediately that no one's missing.'

'How can you tell who's who?' Jake asked, pulling off his anorak and cramming it into his rucksack. With the sun blazing down, it was getting hot and sticky in the forest.

'Well, Bibi's torn ear is a dead giveaway of course,' said David. 'But apart from that, you get to know each chimp very well when you observe them regularly – and they get to know us too!' He ducked out of the way of an enormous flying beetle heading straight for him, then continued. 'Most of the chimps in this forest are used to Richard, Nkonko and me, which is why we can get pretty close to them. They're all very different, in looks as well as personality.'

'Like humans, I suppose,' Jake said, wondering if he'd be able to tell the chimps in Bibi's group apart if he saw them again.

'Absolutely,' said David, unzipping his jacket. He took a swig of water from his flask then put it back in the side flap of his rucksack. 'Right then, everyone. Time to move on.'

For a while, the going was just as tough as before. Jake had to force his way through brambles and creepers, climb over huge fallen tree trunks, and clamber up and down steep, slippery slopes. Once, a bushpig crashed out of a thicket beside him and went hurtling down the hill, and shortly afterwards a troop of baboons crossed right in front of them, barking in alarm when they saw the humans.

From time to time, Richard and Nkonko would stop and call out a chimp greeting. But there was no reply.

'Maybe they're all hiding in another part of the forest, far away from where they heard the shots,'

Jake suggested to Hannah. He stopped to hold back a thorny creeper out of his mum's way.

'Could be,' said Hannah, passing him then holding the end of the vine for Jake. 'But that's not really what David and the scouts are looking for,' she reminded him.

Jake nodded grimly. David and his men were looking for evidence of the attack so they could catch the poachers. But what exactly would that evidence be?

They stopped for lunch in a wide clearing at the top of a hill. To one side, there was a huge tree with spreading branches. It towered above its neighbours. 'I bet there's a good view from up there,' Jake said.

'Let's check it out,' suggested Ross, standing up and brushing the seat of his shorts.

Jake pulled himself up through the branches as high as he could, then wedged himself securely in a fork of the trunk. He looked down at the dense green forest below him. 'It goes on for miles,' he called to Ross who was sitting on a branch just below him.

'Yeah. But look over there,' said Ross, pointing down to the other side of the hill.

The forest was a lot sparser there, and Jake could make out a large banana plantation at the bottom of the slope. Concentrating his gaze, he spotted a narrow path meandering up the side of the hill. Even from a distance, Jake could see it was well worn. 'Do you think the poachers came up that path?' he asked.

'Probably,' answered Ross. 'It's dead easy to get into the forest that way. Dad posts guards up here, but it's such a big area they can't see everything.'

'A chopper would be helpful,' Jake said, thinking about the anti-poaching teams in Tanzania who used helicopters to patrol many of the vast game reserves.

'You bet,' said Ross, his eyes gleaming. 'It's just our luck that Luama's budget doesn't stretch that far.'

David whistled up to them. 'Come on, guys,' he said. 'We'd better get moving again. Otherwise we'll be going home in the dark.'

Jake was about to start down the trunk behind Ross when he spotted another clearing nearby, half hidden by a clump of large bushes. Something about it made Jake look twice. Unlike the other clearings he'd seen that day, the bushes and undergrowth in this one looked squashed and trampled. He craned his neck for a better look and saw a flat, dark object lying on the ground near a rock. His heart missed a beat. It looked just like a panga, the big, broad-bladed knife that was widely used in Africa.

Jake caught his breath. Was this a sign the poachers had been here?

He shinned down the tree, jumping down the last bit and landing on the ground next to Ross. 'There's a panga over there,' he said urgently, pointing towards the other clearing.

David spun round. 'Where?'

'I'll show you,' Jake said, heading towards the clearing. He pushed his way through a mass of thorny bushes, then stopped dead, feeling the blood drain from his face. In the middle of the clearing, among violently flattened bushes, lay the bodies of two dead chimpanzees, their faces set in grimaces of fear and pain.

FOUR

Bloated green flies hovered above the slain chimpanzees, their loud monotonous buzz the only sound. A pair of white-necked ravens dropped heavily to the ground and strutted across the clearing, their beady black eyes fixed on the crumpled heap of limp bodies.

'No!' Jake yelled, unable to help himself. He ran madly towards the scavengers, waving his arms to chase them away.

The ravens flapped their wings and took off into the trees, their high-pitched *kraak-kraak-kraak* breaking the eerie silence. Jake watched the big glossy birds settle on a high branch. He knew they'd be back, but while he was around there was no way he'd let them have a go at the bodies of the chimps.

'They're only doing what comes naturally,' Hannah said gently at Jake's side.

'I know,' Jake said. 'But I don't want to see them

doing it.' Steeling himself, he walked over to the two mangled bodies and looked down at them. One of the chimps was lying on his back, his legs and arms sprawled out at his sides. The other was curled up in a foetal position, one hand clutching a stout stick.

'You poor things,' murmured Hannah, coming up to look at the chimps.

Ross squatted down and stared at the long tapered fingers curled round the makeshift club. 'Were you trying to protect yourself?' he whispered hoarsely.

'It looks like it,' said David, leaning over his shoulder. 'He'd have put up quite a struggle. But no amount of stick-brandishing can stop a gun.' He crouched down and rested one hand on the chimp's side next to a gaping hole where the bullet had entered. Congealed blood surrounded the wound, attracting droves of flies. 'He never stood a chance, poor old boy,' he said.

'Do you know him?' Jake asked, swallowing hard.

David looked at the chimp's lined face. 'I think it's Azizi,' he said. 'The name means treasure.'

'Pity the hunters didn't think he was precious enough to keep alive,' Jake muttered to Nkonko who was kneeling down next to him.

The scout nodded solemnly and pointed to the other dead animal. 'That's his brother, Ambatana. It means stick together.'

'These guys hung out all the time, and only joined up with the A-community every now and then,' put in David.

Ross looked at his dad, frowning. 'I wonder why the hunters left them behind?'

'I'm not sure,' answered David, slowly. 'Maybe because they're both pretty old and haven't got much flesh on them.' Gently, he pushed Azizi over. The bony landed on its back with a soft thud, the mouth jerking open. Jake saw that the old male's teeth were worn down almost to the gums. He gazed at the other dead chimp, which seemed just as ancient, his hair thin and brown, unlike the thick black coats of the B-chimps.

With the antics of Bibi, Baya and the rest of the B-community still fresh in his mind, Jake just couldn't believe that anyone would want to kill such intelligent, human-like creatures. 'If they're too old and tough to be eaten, why kill them?' he asked David.

David was about to answer when Richard called out from the place where Jake had seen the panga. 'Hey! Come and see this.' He was pointing at the big rock.

They all stood up and hurried across the clearing to Richard. Even after the heart-rending sight of the two dead brothers, Jake wasn't prepared for what he saw. The rock and the ground around it were strewn with skins that were still covered in thick black fur. Streaks of dried blood stained the flattened grass, while a muddy red and white striped cloth, equally blood-stained, lay half hidden by a shrub.

Jake rubbed a hand over his eyes.

At his side, Hannah gasped and turned away. 'I can't bear this,' she murmured, her voice choking with emotion. She reached out blindly and gripped Jake's arm, her fingers digging in painfully.

Richard bent down and picked up the cloth, disturbing the multitude of flies that had landed on it. Jake felt his head swim, and Ross muttered an oath. Underneath the cloth, a heap of severed black hands and feet lay in the soggy leaf mould. Jake stared, not wanting to believe his eyes. An entire group of chimpanzees must have been killed here!

He turned to his mother, who was standing ashen-faced, one hand covering her mouth in dismay. 'Why?' he said to her, his fists clenched in angry misery.

Hannah shook her head slowly, tears spilling down her face. She shut her eyes as if trying to block out the horror. 'It looks like a massacre,' she whispered.

Richard dropped the cloth and looked up at David. 'Bad trouble here, eh, *Bwana*? Not just small-time hunters looking for bushmeat for their families.'

'You're right, Richard,' answered David, grimly. 'This is big-scale poaching, by commercial hunters. It looks like they've taken all of the A-group.'

'Except for Azizi and Ambatana,' Ross reminded them. He shooed away a fly that was circling his head. 'I suppose the hunters couldn't carry them all so they left the least valuable ones behind.'

'Where do they sell the meat?' Jake asked, struggling to get his head round the practicalities of the operation.

'In the bigger towns,' replied Ross. 'There's quite a demand there.'

'An entire community of chimps represents a lot of money, especially if there are youngsters among them,' put in David.

'Youngsters?' Jake echoed, feeling the word stick in his throat. 'Do people prefer eating the babies?'

'Oh, they're not eaten,' said David. 'They're sold as pets on the black market. Dealers buy them from hunters then smuggle them abroad.' He bent down to examine the blood-stained panga lying not far from the rock. 'Just one baby chimp fetches a handsome profit, much more than a hunter can earn from selling meat in the local markets.' He took a clean handkerchief out of his pocket and wrapped it round the handle of the bush knife. 'Might as well take this back with us,' he said.

'Do you think you'll be able to find the poachers?' Jake asked hopefully. If their fingerprints were all over the panga then that would almost certainly prove their guilt.

'We'll do our best. But it's usually impossible to trace these people. Even if they leave evidence like this at the scene,' said David, carefully sliding the panga into his rucksack.

Hannah took the lens cap off her camera. 'There's other evidence that's important here,' she said, squinting through the viewfinder and taking a shot of the skins. She was still deathly pale, but her voice was much firmer. 'People who want to buy pet chimps need to see exactly what's involved. It could help to change their minds.' She touched Richard's arm. 'Would you mind holding up that cloth again?'

Richard lifted the blood-soaked rag. Hannah looked away for a moment. She took a deep breath to compose herself, then, pursing her lips with determination, she snapped several close-ups of the grisly pile of hands and feet. Next she moved across to the two corpses in the middle of the clearing, chasing away the ravens which had settled on the forest floor next to the chimps.

While Hannah photographed the tragic scene,

David tried to contact Liz to tell her about their discovery. But they were out of range of the other radio receiver. 'We'll just have to wait until we're back at camp to inform the police,' he said. He took one more look round the clearing. 'Well, we found what we set out to find.' With the back of his hand he wiped beads of perspiration off his brow. 'We might as well head out of here now. There's nothing more we can do for these fellows.' He heaved his rucksack on to his back, looking drained and exhausted.

A low *kurrr* sounded in a tree above. Jake looked up. The two ravens were waiting restlessly on a branch. 'Hold on!' he blurted out, feeling sick. 'Can't we bury the bodies?'

David stopped. 'Well it's not really necessary—' he began, but Ross interrupted him.

'Good idea, Jake,' he said, dumping his backpack on the ground. 'It's the least we can do for them.'

'But we haven't got a shovel,' said Nkonko.

'Yes, we have,' said Ross. 'Sort of.' He picked up a stone that had a pointed end and started digging into the soft forest floor with it. 'Chimps use stones as tools all the time, so we can make our own spades, too.'

'Well, OK,' said David. 'But it'll take a long time to dig a big enough hole.'

'Not if we all help,' Ross insisted, jabbing at the soil.

Jake put down his backpack and looked round for a stone. There was nothing close by so he walked to the edge of the clearing, scrutinizing the ground for something suitable for digging. He picked up and rejected a small rock that was too round to make any impact on the ground. He glanced across at the others. They'd all found implements and were busily scraping at Ross's shallow hole. Hannah had found a sturdy log while Nkonko was using an enamel cup from his rucksack. David and Richard were using sharp-ended stones like Ross.

I have to find something, Jake thought, feeling in his pocket. His hand closed round his Swiss army knife. He flicked open the blade. 'Better than nothing, I suppose,' he muttered, and turned to join the others.

Just then, he heard a faint whimpering sound in the bushes behind him. Catching his breath, he stood very still and waited. *Hoo*, came the soft whimper again.

Instinctively, Jake imitated the quiet call. '*Hoo*,' he breathed without moving.

Hoo, hoo, came the subdued sound from the trees behind him. It was the faintest of cries, but it was enough for Jake to recognize that it belonged to a chimpanzee.

Jake turned very quietly. '*Hoo, hoo*,' he panted again.

There was a tiny rustling just ahead. With his heart pounding, Jake tiptoed towards the noise. A twig cracked beneath his feet and he stopped dead, anxious that he might have frightened whatever it was hiding in the forest in front of him. He waited for a moment then called out softly again.

This time there was no response. Jake listened hard and thought he heard another muffled rustle. There was a tiny movement underneath a thick bush. Cautiously, he crept towards it then parted the leaves and peered into the middle of the bush.

Staring straight up at him from among the leaves was the pink face of a young chimpanzee, a look of sheer terror in its clear, bright eyes.

'It's OK. It's OK,' Jake whispered, wondering what to do. If he called out to David, the chimp might go scooting away in panic. Its trust in humans was bound to be at an all time low right now. 'I'm not a hunter. I won't hurt you,' Jake murmured, hardly moving his lips. He searched his mind, desperate for a way of showing the chimpanzee he meant it no harm. Then he remembered how Richard had approached Bibi that morning. Slowly, he let go of the branches and sat down, hugging his knees close to his chest to make himself look as small and unthreatening as possible. *'Hoo, hoo,'* he breathed softly, hoping he sounded at least a bit like a friendly chimpanzee.

With his head tucked in, he couldn't see anything, but he was conscious of the chimp staring at him through the bush. He could almost feel the little creature's fear as it sat trembling in its hiding place. Jake waited, frozen to the spot. Would the chimp trust him, or would it obey its terrified instincts and vanish into the forest?

FIVE

'Jake, where are you?' Hannah's voice echoed through the forest.

Before Jake knew it, the little chimpanzee shot out from under the bush and leapfrogged on to his back. Startled, Jake sat bolt upright. The chimp wrapped its strong, hairy arms round his neck and dug its feet uncomfortably into Jake's ribs.

'Hey! Jake!' came Hannah's voice again.

Jake felt the clammy, leathery hands and prehensile feet cling more tightly to him. 'I'm here, Mum,' he said in a hoarse whisper.

Hannah couldn't have heard his feeble reply because she called out a third time, her voice now edged with anxiety. 'Jake! Are you all right?' This was followed by the sound of boots tramping through the leaf mould towards Jake.

He felt the chimpanzee stiffen on his back then, as the footsteps came closer, the little creature began to whimper. 'It's OK. It's OK,' he murmured, feeling at a complete loss. What exactly did a person do with a terrified chimp sticking to him like superglue?

Jake eased himself on to his knees then tried to stand up, but the chimpanzee frantically clambered further up his back and sat on his shoulders, its arms wrapped round his head and its hands covering his face. Knocked off balance, Jake sank back down on to his knees, steadying himself with one hand. 'Hey, you, I can't see a thing,' he muttered as the chimp's fingers pressed down on his eyelids.

He took hold of one of the chimp's hands and managed to prise it away from his eyes just in time to see Hannah and David coming through from the clearing.

'There you—' began Hannah, before her voice was drowned out by the chimpanzee's sudden frantic screams.

Astonished, David stopped in his tracks and said something that Jake couldn't hear, then came forward more slowly.

The chimpanzee slipped down from Jake's shoulders and gripped his neck again, almost strangling him, all the while screaming deafeningly in his left ear. Jake tried to loosen one of the shaggy arms so that he could breathe, but the distraught animal tightened its hold even more. 'Could somebody help me out here?' Jake managed to croak between shrieks. He shot his mum a desperate look.

But Hannah ignored his plea. 'The poor baby's terrified!' she said to David as the hysterical screaming subsided into whimpering. 'It must have escaped from the hunters.'

'Looks like it,' said David. He came forward again, crooning softly to the petrified young chimp. 'Come on, little one. Let's see who you are.'

But the infant was taking no chances. Grunting nervously, it swung round from Jake's back and clung to his chest like a leech, pressing its hairless face into his neck. Jake could feel hot puffs of chimp breath against his skin. He could also smell the chimp for the first time. It was a strong, wild, unwashed sort of smell that made him want to cover his nose. Slowly, he rose to his feet, one arm supporting the chimp's back. He frowned at David. 'Now what?' he asked.

David said nothing, just gazed at the trembling chimp, his eyes soft with concern. Then he reached out with one hand and gently smoothed its back. The chimp half-turned its head and glanced at David. It seemed to recognize him because it pushed its lip forward in a pout, gave two soft pant-hoots, then turned to burrow its face into Jake's neck again.

The cracking of sticks underfoot signalled the arrival of Ross and the two scouts.

'Hey! What are you guys up to?' asked Ross. 'We've done all the—' He stopped dead when he saw the chimpanzee clinging to Jake. 'Well, how about that!' he exclaimed quietly. 'One of the babies is alive. Do you know who it is, Dad?'

'Not yet,' replied David. 'She's a young female and very traumatized. But that's all I can tell you until she lets me have a good look at her.'

'Let's see if she'll accept this,' suggested Hannah, taking a banana out of her pocket and going to stand next to Jake. 'She's probably starving.' The shivering infant shot a furtive, sidelong glance at her.

'Go on. Take it,' urged Hannah, holding out the banana.

Unable to resist the tasty fruit, the chimp lifted one trembling hand and grabbed the banana quickly. With her huge eyes fixed on Hannah's face, she hastily peeled off the skin with her teeth, then stuffed the whole banana into her mouth.

'There,' soothed Hannah. 'That's better, isn't it?'

Jake felt the chimpanzee relax against him as she chewed. Her grip round his neck eased and her body stopped trembling. When she finished, she reached towards Hannah, her hand turned upwards in a begging gesture.

'Oh, I'm sorry, baby,' said Hannah. 'There's no more.'

The chimp blinked shyly but kept her hand stretched out.

'OK, then. What about this?' asked Hannah, taking a half-eaten egg sandwich out of her backpack. She offered it to the chimp who snatched it at once.

Meanwhile, David and the scouts were observing the infant.

'She's one of the older babies,' announced Nkonko after a while. 'Asali's little one, I think.'

'In that case she's about three years old,' said David. 'Not nearly old enough to fend for herself. She'll have to come back to camp with us.' He patted her gently on one shoulder.

The chimpanzee let out a single, sharp shriek and jerked away from David's touch, lurching round to cling to Jake's side. Jake found himself staggering slightly. It was as if a jolt of electricity had shot through the chimp. Whimpering miserably, she sat on Jake's hip, her whole body shaking.

'What was that all about?' Jake asked, frowning down at her. He noticed a matted clump of hair on the shoulder David had touched. Looking closer, he saw that the fur was crusted with dried blood. 'Hey. I think she's been shot,' he said.

David peered closely at the injury without touching it again. The chimp blinked nervously. 'It's definitely a gunshot wound,' David said. 'Luckily, it looks like the bullet just grazed her shoulder. We'll have to keep an eye on it and make sure it doesn't get infected.'

Hannah was taking more photographs. 'Poor little soul,' she said, lowering her camera. 'Can you imagine what she's been through?'

Jake tried to picture the scene in the clearing. 'She probably saw her mother being butchered,' he said, stumbling over the words.

'And if that wasn't bad enough, she found herself all alone when the hunters finally left,' said Ross.

David was gazing at the trees around them. 'She'd have been as scared as any three-year-old child who was lost,' he said, craning his neck to look up into the branches of one tall tree. He took a few steps backward then pointed up the massive trunk. 'See that?'

Jake craned his neck. David was pointing to an upright fork half hidden by leafy branches.

'That's a chimp's nest,' David explained. 'You can see how they've bent all the surrounding branches down into the fork.'

'Oh, right!' Jake said, realizing that he was looking at a leafy green bed built into the fork of the tree. 'Do you think she was up there when the hunters attacked the rest of the community?' he asked David.

'Probably,' said David. 'Maybe her mother, Asali, was in the nest with her when the gang arrived. They might have seen the adult and shot her in the tree.'

'Which could account for the bullet grazing the baby's shoulder,' Hannah suggested.

'Right,' put in David. 'She might have been hiding behind her mother. When Asali fell to the ground, the hunters would have made a beeline for her and not bothered to look for anyone else in the nest.' Slowly, he reached for the chimp. 'But whatever happened, at least there's one survivor. Come on, little one,' he said, trying to lift her off Jake's hip. 'Let's take you back to camp.'

The infant recoiled in terror. She clung to Jake's neck and squeaked pitifully.

'All right,' David soothed. 'I won't take you away from him.' He smiled at Jake. 'I guess she's adopted you as her foster mother! Can you manage to carry her all the way back?'

'I think so,' Jake said uncertainly. He remembered with a wince the punishing slopes and dense bush they'd struggled through that morning. How was he going to make his way through all of that with a chimp on his hip?

They returned to the clearing to fetch their rucksacks, Jake holding the chimp in his arms. He didn't think he'd have to worry about dropping her

– she was clinging so tightly he wondered if she would ever let go.

'I'll carry your rucksack,' Ross offered. 'You've got enough on your back as it is!'

In single file, they started back for the camp. Nkonko led as he'd done that morning, while Richard walked at the back. Jake followed David, with Ross and Hannah coming behind him.

'What'll happen to her?' Jake asked David as they picked their way slowly down the first steep slope. 'Will she be able to go back to the forest one day?'

David shrugged without looking round. 'In a perfect world, yes. The trouble is, communities of chimps aren't that willing to adopt outsiders, even if they're infants. It's quite possible she'll have to go to a smaller sanctuary where rescued chimps are kept in enclosures because they wouldn't survive on their own in the wild.'

'Surely not!' said Hannah, drawing level with Jake at the bottom of the slope. 'She's been free for three years – anything else would feel like captivity to her.'

'I don't like the idea myself,' said David heavily. 'But without a maternal figure, she'd never cope out here. At this age, young chimps are very dependent on their mothers for security and comfort, even if they're reasonably independent in other ways.'

'What a terrible wrench it's going to be for her,' said Hannah, stroking the chimp's head. 'She's lost everything.'

They trekked across a wide clearing, climbing over a number of fallen tree trunks, before finding themselves among dense bushes and tangled undergrowth again. By now, Jake was feeling the full weight of the chimp on his hip. He guessed she probably only weighed about ten kilograms, like a sack of potatoes, but carrying any extra weight over such rough terrain was heavy going.

'How about walking on your own for a while?' Jake puffed when they found themselves at the top of another rugged hill. He leaned over to one side, hoping the chimp would drop to the ground. 'Come on,' Jake urged, trying to loosen her grip on his shoulder.

But the chimpanzee clearly didn't want to get down. She clung on with all her might, whimpering unhappily until Jake straightened up again.

'You're a dead-weight, you know,' he muttered, starting down the slope. Beneath his feet, the mushy wet leaves were as slippery as ice. He turned sideways and continued, crab-like, down the hill. Every now and then he lost his footing and had to grab on to a branch, or sometimes even sink to the ground to stop himself from sliding to the bottom. 'I wish you'd take a shine to Ross for a bit,' he said when he was safely on level ground again.

'Don't worry,' Ross grinned. 'I've had my fair share of that kind of thing, with a chimp called Mtoto about six years ago. It was weeks before she'd let anyone else handle her.'

'Weeks!' Jake echoed faintly. He didn't think he could handle this kind of close relationship for that long!

They stopped to rest beside a pool below a waterfall that plunged down a narrow cleft in a cliff. Tiny birds and colourful butterflies flitted in and out of the fine spray. With the chimp still on his hip, Jake sat on the edge of a flat rock and dangled his legs in the cool water.

'Swim, anyone?' said Ross, taking off his T-shirt before plunging into the cool depths.

Jake thought that was a great idea. 'This is definitely where you get off,' he said to the chimpanzee. 'Or else you're coming in for a dip too!' With his free hand, he fished around in his bag for some food. 'How about some peanuts?' He tossed the packet a little way from him. The chimp eyed it eagerly then let go of Jake and scampered over to the nuts.

Grabbing the opportunity, Jake slid straight off the rock into the pool. 'Just what I needed!' he grinned to Ross who was floating blissfully on his back. Jake called across to Hannah who was leaning against a tree. 'Coming in, Mum?'

'No, thanks,' responded Hannah. 'You never know what else might be in there!'

Jake was too hot to care about that. It was just brilliant to be able to cool off. Feeling his T-shirt ballooning around him, Jake peeled it off and tossed it on to the rocks. It landed right next to where the chimpanzee was sitting as she gobbled down the peanuts, all the while keeping a close eye on Jake.

'Look after that for me,' Jake joked and to his surprise, the chimpanzee grabbed the soggy shirt and held on to it.

'Is that your security blanket, little chimp?' laughed David as he and the two scouts took off their shirts and slipped into the pool too.

'Let's give her a name,' suggested Hannah, pulling off her boots and gingerly dangling her feet in the water.

'It'll have to start with A,' Ross reminded her.

Jake couldn't help wondering if this was important now that the A-community had been wiped out. But perhaps it was, as a sort of memorial to the others. 'Any ideas?' he asked Ross who was treading water next to him.

'Well,' began Ross. 'There's, um, *Adha*,' he grinned.

'What does that mean?' Jake asked.

'Trouble,' said Ross.

Jake wrinkled his nose. 'She's not really trouble, just a dead-weight!' He looked at the chimp who was watching them with huge wary eyes. 'A shy dead-weight,' he added.

'Then let's call her *Ashai*,' suggested Ross. 'It means shy.'

'That's cool!' Jake said. 'What do you think of that, Ashai?'

The chimp pouted and draped one of her arms across her face, peering at them over the top of it.

'Look at that,' laughed Hannah. 'I think she understands what you're talking about!'

When it was time to set off again, Jake hauled himself on to the ledge and tried to take back his T-shirt. Ashai refused to let him have it. She pushed it under her arm then lowered her eyes and blinked at Jake. 'Oh, all right,' Jake said. 'You can keep it. It's too soggy to put on anyway.'

The others shouldered their rucksacks and began to walk away. Jake waited, expecting Ashai to jump on to his back again. To his surprise, though, she just grabbed his hand tightly then, as Jake set off, she tottered along next to him on her back legs, rocking from side to side like an unsteady toddler.

'That's better,' said Jake, feeling hugely relieved.

Darkness was falling when they arrived back at

camp. Liz came running out to meet them. 'I was getting worried,' she began, then her mouth dropped open as she spotted Ashai loping along next to Jake. 'Who's this?'

'Let's have a drink in the boma and we'll tell you all about her,' David said, wearily dropping his rucksack to the ground.

'We'll need more than one drink,' said Ross. 'There's lots to tell.'

That night, Jake lay awake in bed listening to Ashai whimpering in the holding pen next door. She'd had a meal of fruit and seemed quite happy at first to settle down in the soft leafy bed that Jake and Ross had made for her. But as soon as Jake left the enclosure with Ross, Ashai began to cry. Forcing himself not to look back at her, Jake had walked away quickly. It had been tough, but Jake had learned enough about Africa's wild animals to know that if Ashai stood any chance of living a natural life, she couldn't depend on him.

Now, however, hearing Ashai's distressed cries, he just couldn't ignore her any longer. *Maybe I'll go and calm her down just this once*, Jake decided, getting out of bed.

He pulled on his sandals and grabbed his torch then went out to the enclosure. As soon as Ashai saw him, she stopped whimpering and began to grunt softly. '*Hoo, hoo,*' she panted between grunts, her head to one side as she watched Jake opening the gate.

'Ssh,' Jake whispered. He slipped inside and Ashai came tumbling over to him, grunting gleefully. She leaped into his arms and snuggled up against his chest.

Jake smoothed the back of her head, just as if she were a fractious baby. 'I'm not supposed to be here,' he murmured. 'So I'm just spending a few minutes with you and then you must go back to bed.' He yawned hugely. After trekking through the forest for twelve hours, he was exhausted.

Imitating him, Ashai opened her mouth and yawned, finishing with a low-pitched grunt.

'You look worn out, too,' Jake said, carrying her back to her bed. He bent down to put her in the nest, but she wrapped her arms stubbornly round his neck and refused to let go.

'Not again!' Jake sighed, trying to unclasp her rigid hands. He managed to release one of them but Ashai instantly let out a loud shriek and grabbed his hair.

'Ouch!' Jake winced as Ashai yanked hard. 'That hurts! And stop screaming like that, you'll wake up the whole camp.' He sat down on the damp ground next to her bed, hoping she'd give up and nestle down again. But Ashai clung to him, her bottom lip pushed forward in a pout. 'If you'd been from an R-community, we could have called you *Ruba*,' said Jake, remembering the word for leech that his friend Shani had taught him.

After a while, Ashai calmed down. She nuzzled into Jake's neck, grunting softly. But Jake knew that the minute he tried to leave her, she'd go crazy again! He realized he had no choice. 'OK, here's the deal,' he said, standing up and carrying her over to the gate. 'You can sleep in my tent, but just for tonight. And you'd better let me put you back in here first thing in the morning before everyone wakes up. Otherwise I'll be in big trouble.'

SIX

Back in his tent, Jake put a spare pillow on the floor next to the bed. 'You can sleep here,' he said, putting Ashai down. To his relief, she uncurled her arms from his neck and squatted on the floor, blinking. Jake patted the pillow. 'Come on, bed time,' he urged.

Ashai inspected the pillow inquisitively then lay face down on it with her bottom in the air. Jake flopped on to his bed, pulled the mosquito net around him and switched off his torch.

'*Ooph!*' Jake felt the air being squashed from his lungs as Ashai landed heavily on his chest, yanking the mosquito net down from the hooks in the roof of the tent. 'Now look here,' Jake said, untangling himself from the net then gently pushing Ashai off him. 'You're supposed to sleep on the floor.' He sat up and tried to ease her back on to the pillow. Ashai clung to his arm, whimpering pitifully.

'I'm not going anywhere,' Jake said impatiently. He kicked the rumpled mosquito net to the bottom of his bed. 'And if it helps, I'll lie with my arm dangling down like this. You can hold on to it all night if you must.'

Ashai sat on the pillow, holding his wrist with her little black fingers and staring up at him.

'See. I'm still here,' Jake said, lying on his side and facing her. 'You're quite safe now, I promise.'

For a while, Ashai was very still. Jake felt her grip on his arm slacken. *Good*, he thought to himself. *She's settled down at last.* He started to drift off to sleep but suddenly he was wide awake again, struggling to breathe through a mass of shaggy fur.

'Ashai!' he said crossly, pushing her away from his face. She'd sneaked back on to his bed and spread herself over his head.

Jake felt defeated. Ashai was determined to be as close to him as possible. 'I guess it's how you slept in the nest with your mother,' he said with a sigh. He rolled on to his back and Ashai snuggled up at his side, one long arm draped over his chest.

'All right,' Jake said, smoothing her head. 'But just keep still. And don't suffocate me again.'

For the rest of the night, Ashai slept soundly next to Jake, at peace for the first time since the attack. But Jake had a much less restful night. With the mosquito net a crumpled heap at the foot of his bed, he was plagued by the insects whining round him. He couldn't see them in the dark, but he could feel them biting his legs, arms and face. It was almost as bad as when the ferry had passed through the swarm of water flies on Lake Victoria two nights ago.

And then there was the matter of the chimpanzee curled up close to him. In the hot tropical night, Ashai's hairy body was like an unnecessary electric blanket. Before long, Jake was sweating. He moved carefully away from her until he was lying on the edge of the narrow bed, but Ashai simply shuffled up against him again. This time, she tucked her head snugly under his chin so that wafts of chimp odour drifted up his nose.

'Thanks a lot!' Jake grimaced, turning over. For a minute he was tempted to sleep on the floor, but he knew he'd end up being even more uncomfortable. Besides, Ashai was bound to join him.

Eventually, Jake's exhaustion won and he fell into a deep sleep just as the sky was beginning to grow light.

Loud anxious voices outside woke Jake up. He felt groggy, as if he'd only just gone to sleep. He opened his eyes to find Ashai sitting on her haunches next to him, peering at his face. 'Morning, Ashai,' he muttered. 'I expect *you* slept well last night.'

Outside, the voices became more urgent. Rubbing his eyes, Jake sat up. It dawned on him that someone must have discovered that Ashai wasn't in the enclosure. 'Oops! I'm for it now,' he groaned, glancing at his wristwatch. After his late night, he'd slept longer than he'd meant to. 'You should have been back in your own bed ages ago,' he said to Ashai. 'I guess we'd better go and face the music.' He grabbed his clothes and had just finished dressing when the tent flap was pushed aside.

Hannah appeared in the doorway. 'Bad news—' she began, but then she spotted Ashai sitting on Jake's bed, fidgeting with the mosquito net. 'Oh, thank goodness!' she said. She looked back over her shoulder and called out, 'It's OK, Liz. Ashai's in here with Jake.' Then she came into the tent, looking cross. 'You've got a lot of explaining to do, Jake. Everyone's been worried sick about Ashai. What on earth are you playing at?'

'Sorry, Mum,' Jake said. 'It's just that she was so upset last night and—'

'You thought you'd comfort her,' Hannah interrupted.

'Yes. That's exactly what happened,' Jake admitted.

Meanwhile, Ashai had pulled the net over her head and was peering at them through the mesh. Jake thought she looked very comical and completely relaxed. 'It worked,' he said quickly to his mum, defending himself. 'Look how calm she is now. I bet if I'd left her in the enclosure she'd still be a nervous wreck.'

Hannah gave him a sideways glance. 'I don't know about that,' she said. 'You might have made things worse by letting her get more attached to you.'

'I know,' Jake said ruefully. 'But I didn't know what else to do. You should have heard her going on in there.'

Hannah sighed. 'I suppose you thought you were doing the right thing. But next time, don't be so impulsive. Consider the bigger picture first.' She went over to the bed and crouched down in front of Ashai. 'Feeling better today?' she asked softly.

Shyly, Ashai pulled the net off her head. She gazed at Hannah, her lips apart so that her front teeth showed in a coy grin.

'She's smiling at you,' Jake said.

'I suppose she is,' chuckled Hannah.

Ashai frowned and made a soft grunting noise then timidly reached out and began playing with the gold chain round Hannah's neck. It was the first time the chimp had tried to touch anyone other than Jake.

'Er, I'm very flattered,' said Hannah, leaning backwards then standing up. 'But I'd rather you didn't fiddle with that.'

'*Hoo*,' whimpered Ashai, pouting with frustration. She stood on the bed, reaching up with her long arms to grab the chain again.

'No, you don't,' said Hannah, quickly taking off the necklace and hiding it in her pocket. But Ashai grabbed Hannah's hand and tugged at it while jumping up and down on the bed. Jake thought she was behaving just like a spoilt child. No wonder young chimps needed their mothers for so long! They didn't grow up any more quickly than humans.

The tent flap parted again and Liz came in, followed by Ross. 'Phew!' she breathed. 'We were beginning to think the poachers had found her. How did she get in here?'

'Well,' Jake began, feeling rather embarrassed. He explained what he'd done. 'I know I shouldn't have interfered, but it seemed like the best thing to do at the time,' he finished.

Liz smiled at him. 'Don't beat yourself up about it,' she said. 'Especially as Ashai is so much happier today.' The chimpanzee had climbed on to Hannah's hip and was inspecting her earrings. 'I think the most important thing is for Ashai to recover from her ordeal. After all, we can't even think about finding a new home for her until she's feeling secure again.'

'So you want us to spend a lot of time with her?' asked Ross, reaching over to stroke Ashai's head.

'Well, not all day,' said Liz. 'Maybe an hour or two at a time so that she doesn't get bored and lonely. Just don't make her too dependent on you.'

'OK. How about if we teach her some chimp skills?' said Ross. 'Like termiting. After all, it's what her mother would have been doing.'

Liz laughed. 'You can try. But I don't think you'll have much luck before we have to find a permanent home for her. It takes a chimp hours of practice to learn how to catch ants.'

'Well, as her foster – er – *mothers*, we'll just have to do our best,' Jake chuckled.

With Hannah carrying Ashai, they all went over to the boma for breakfast. The camp cook brought out a big bowl of fruit and set it down on the ground next to Jake's chair. Ashai's eyes lit up when she saw it. Grunting with pleasure, she clambered down from Hannah's hip and sat hunched over the dish, chomping a guava with a blissful look on her face.

'Nothing wrong with her appetite,' grinned David.

'There never was,' Hannah reminded him. 'Even in her shocked state yesterday she still took that banana from me.'

'Let's hope her resilience pays off when we decide what to do with her,' said David. He watched Ashai spitting out some date pips. 'I just hope she doesn't get too used to the good life here,' he added.

After breakfast, Ross suggested to Jake that they start Ashai's training straight away. 'There's an active termites' nest just in front of the main tent,' he said.

The nest was marked by an enormous mound of compacted earth that the ants had excavated over many seasons. Loose beads of soil around the hole at the top of the heap revealed fresh activity among the worker ants.

'What do we do?' Jake asked Ross as they crouched next to the nest. Ashai sat down beside them and poked at a shiny black beetle with her index finger.

'First we need a tool to put in the hole,' answered Ross. 'Like this.' He picked a grass stem then slowly pushed it into the nest.

'Now what?' said Jake.

'Wait until some ants are crawling up the grass, then take it out.'

'And eat them?'

'Of course,' grinned Ross. 'Ants are delicious.'

Nearby, Ashai was showing no interest in the ant-fishing lesson. She had climbed into a small tree and was swinging from a low branch.

'Hey! You're supposed to be watching this so that you can start fending for yourself,' Jake scolded. He turned to watch Ross again. How hard could it be, catching a few ants on a piece of grass?

Concentrating hard, Ross held the grass stalk very still. After a few minutes, he slowly pulled it out. It was empty! 'Lesson number one,' Ross laughed. 'You have to be patient. But the chimps make it look so easy.'

He slid the stem back in to the hole. Jake plucked a stalk from a clump of grass and inserted it into the nest beside Ross's grass. He tried to look inside the tunnel, but it was too dark. 'How do you know if an ant climbs on your stick?' he asked Ross.

'Dunno,' answered Ross. 'You just guess, I suppose.'

Suddenly Jake felt a sharp, painful nip on his hand. A big ant had come out and sunk its pincers into the skin between his thumb and index finger. 'Yikes!' Jake yelled, shaking the termite off.

Ross burst out laughing. 'You're supposed to eat the ant. Not the other way round!'

'At least I caught one – sort of,' Jake joked back, glancing at the empty stalk that Ross was drawing out from the tunnel.

Hannah and Liz were watching them from the deck of the main tent. 'Pretty feeble attempts so far,' chuckled Liz. 'I don't think Ashai is going to learn a whole lot from you two!'

'Give us a chance,' retorted Ross, pushing his grass stalk into the nest again.

Ashai had climbed higher into her tree and was peering down at them from a branch that overhung the nest. She hooted at them once as if to get their attention, then swung down from the bough, landing nearby with a thud.

'About time too,' Jake said as Ashai sidled up to him. 'This is all for your benefit, you know.'

'*Hoo, hoo, waa*,' hooted Ashai, her forehead wrinkled in a frown as if she was bewildered by what they were doing.

'*Hoo* to you too,' Jake smiled. 'You've got to learn stuff like this you know.'

With a serious expression on her face, Ashai looked at Ross's stalk, then examined the one in Jake's hand. Grunting softly, she took it away from him.

'Hey! That's mine. Find your own,' Jake protested as Ashai shuffled closer to the nest and began fishing for ants.

It wasn't long before a couple of termites came running up Ashai's piece of grass. Carefully, the chimpanzee lifted her makeshift tool out of the nest then deftly picked off the ants with her rubbery lips while giving Jake an almost smug look from under her eyebrows.

'OK, I get it,' Jake laughed, amused by the twinkle in Ashai's eyes. 'You're the real expert around here.'

'Who's teaching who?' laughed Hannah from the deck, quickly taking a photograph.

'Talking about learning,' called Liz, 'shouldn't you be doing some studying, Ross? You didn't do any yesterday.'

Unlike Jake who went to school in Dar es Salaam, Ross was home-schooled.

Ross groaned. 'I guess so.' He stood up and dusted off his hands. 'Exams looming,' he told Jake.

'And I'm supposed to do a report on chimps for school,' Jake said. 'That's how I managed to get a week off.'

Ross called up to his mum. 'We'll just put Ashai back in her enclosure.'

'Why don't Jake and I do it?' suggested Hannah, coming down from the deck. 'I'd like to get some close-up pictures of her.' She reached out to Ashai but the chimp ignored her and grabbed Jake's hand instead. 'Snubbed by a chimp!' laughed Hannah as they made their way to the enclosure.

Opening the gate, Jake wondered if Ashai would mind being back in the pen. But the chimp seemed unfazed and happily went in with him to pose for some photos.

Hannah took a few more shots then she and Jake turned to go.

'See you later, Ashai,' Jake called as he swung the gate behind him and pulled the bolt across. But the second he turned his back, Ashai broke out screaming.

'Oh, come on, Ashai,' Jake groaned. 'I can't stay with you all the time.' He looked back at her, then froze. 'Don't move, Ashai,' he yelled, grabbing the bolt on the gate.

'What's the matter?' asked Hannah.

'Snake!' Jake cried.

Just metres from Ashai, a thick brown snake was gliding across the enclosure. It was heading straight for her.

'Don't!' said Hannah, grabbing Jake's arm and pulling him away from the gate. 'It's too dangerous. I'll get help.' She raced off towards the office tent.

Inside the enclosure, Ashai started to scream even more frantically. Appalled, Jake saw the snake moving closer to her. In the blink of an eye, it reared up, showing its black-barred neck as it spread its hood. It was ready to strike!

'No!' Jake shouted. He jerked the bolt across then pushed open the gate and hurtled across the enclosure, pulling Ashai away just as the snake struck. A burst of deadly venom shot out from the snake's gaping jaws, missing Ashai by a few millimetres.

The enraged snake dropped to the ground. Out of breath, Jake stared at it, expecting it to come at them again. But the snake slithered away, past the spot where Ashai had been sitting just seconds before, and disappeared through the fence into the thick bush beyond.

Jake tried to swallow, but his mouth was dry. 'That was close,' he croaked. Ashai clung to his hip, whimpering in fear. 'It's OK. It's OK,' Jake said, trying to calm her down. But, trembling uncontrollably, he felt anything but calm himself.

Moments later, Hannah came running back with David and Nkonko. 'I told you not to go in there, Jake,' she said angrily when she saw him standing in the middle of the enclosure. 'What if the snake had struck you?'

Jake looked down at the ground. 'I didn't think about that,' he muttered.

'Didn't I warn you earlier about being too impulsive?' Hannah reminded him. 'You can't just go jumping into situations like that.'

Jake nodded but said nothing. He'd had no choice really. He would never have forgiven himself if the snake had hurt Ashai.

David came over to Jake. 'What did the snake look like?'

Jake described it.

'Sounds like a spitting cobra,' said David. 'Nasty snake, that. You were lucky. It could have blinded Ashai – and you too if you hadn't been so quick.'

Hearing this, Hannah put an arm round Jake's shoulder. 'It was a pretty daft thing to do. But I guess you saved Ashai,' she said quietly. 'Next time though, try to think before you act.'

'I'll try,' Jake promised, meeting her blue-eyed gaze and grinning.

SEVEN

'What about the panga? Won't the cops want that too?' Jake asked Ross.

'Oops! Nearly forgot it,' said Ross, leaping down from the jeep and heading back to the tents.

It was after breakfast the next morning. Liz was going to Baguru, the nearest town, to deliver David's report on the chimpanzee massacre to the police. She also needed to stock up on supplies, so Jake, Ross and Hannah were going along to help out. David was staying behind to keep an eye on Ashai and the camp.

Ross came back with the panga inside a brown paper bag. He put it on the back seat between him and Jake. 'It probably wouldn't have made any difference if we had forgotten it,' he said as Liz started up the engine.

'Why not?' Jake asked, puzzled. As far as he was concerned, a blood-stained knife covered in fingerprints had to be hugely important in solving a case.

'Because everyone's got pangas,' said Ross. 'Finding the owner of one as ordinary as this will be like searching for a needle in a haystack. And fingerprints won't mean a thing unless the cops have some suspects.'

'Even the report is just a formality really,' put in Liz, sounding resigned. 'At the end of the day, the best we can do is to keep patrolling Luama's boundaries to make it harder for the poachers.'

It was mid-morning when they reached Baguru. It was a small, busy town with market stalls spilling off the pavements into the narrow streets. Jake had seen similar places in Tanzania but none as packed as this one. Bartering shoppers clustered around the street merchants, blocking the roads and making it almost impossible to drive through the town. Every minute or so, Liz had to stop for pedestrians who stepped out right in front of the jeep. She also had to keep an eye out for other vehicles driving on the wrong side of the road as they, too, tried to avoid people, livestock and small children chasing each other through the lurching traffic. They came to a halt next to a pair of huge amplifiers in front of a stall.

'What a din!' Jake winced, blocking his ears with

his hands. Distorted music blared out, clashing with the tunes blasting from other enormous speakers lining the street. Added to this was the constant honking of horns as frustrated drivers sat with their hands on their hooters while swearing impatiently at each other out of their windows. In the midst of all the hubbub, tiny babies slept soundly on their mothers' backs, as if no amount of noise could disturb them.

Liz was looking for somewhere to leave the jeep. Eventually, she gave up. 'Why don't I drop you and Jake here with the shopping list?' she said to Ross. 'You can get the supplies while Hannah and I go to the police station.'

'OK,' said Ross. 'Do you want us to come down to the station when we've got everything?'

'No. You'll have a job to carry it all. We'll come back for you,' said Liz, giving Ross the shopping list and a wad of bank notes. 'We'll meet you somewhere round here, so keep an eye out for us.' She stopped the jeep and Jake and Ross climbed out. 'You'll need these,' she added, passing several large canvas carrier bags to them before driving on again.

Jake and Ross watched the jeep inch along the choked-up street. 'At this rate, we'll be able to buy all the stuff and catch up with them before they're out of sight!' joked Ross.

'Let's give it a go,' Jake said. But just then there was a gap in the traffic and the jeep disappeared round a bend.

Jake and Ross studied the list. It read: *Vegetables (any); 5 litres paraffin; 4 packets candles; cold drinks (any); 8 soap; 10 kg powdered milk; 5 kg flour; 2 litres oil; batteries (if available); tins – beans, condensed milk, fish, jam, tomatoes; maize meal; 3 dozen eggs.* The last item was: *fruit – lots!*

Jake and Ross stared at the piece of paper.

'She's got to be joking!' exclaimed Ross. 'We can't lug this lot around until she comes back for us.'

'Can't we just wait outside the shop with it all?' Jake asked, picturing a general store selling everything, like the one in the town near his home in Tanzania.

'Which shop?' replied Ross. He gestured up and down the street at the small hut-like buildings on either side. 'They all sell different things. We'll have to go into just about every one to buy all this stuff.'

Jake groaned. 'So where do we begin?'

'With the lightest things, like soap and candles,' said Ross, starting down the pavement. 'We'll leave the big stuff for last.'

Halfway down the street, they came across a merchant sitting on the ground on a straw mat, surrounded by heaps of bananas. Jake immediately thought about Ashai. 'Should we get some of these?' he asked, pausing in front of the man who looked up hopefully at him.

'I guess so,' said Ross. He asked the man for his price, then bartered with him until they were both satisfied with the amount.

'This should keep Ashai going for a while,' Jake said, putting a huge bunch of nearly ripe bananas in one of the canvas bags which he slung over his shoulder.

'Yeah. About ten minutes!' grinned Ross, counting out the correct money and giving it to the merchant.

A few stalls further on, Jake stopped and stared, feeling bile rise in his throat. Blackened lumps of meat were piled on an upturned wooden crate. Blue and green flies swarmed around, some of them landing on the meat before the trader flicked them idly away with a fly swat.

The stall holder smiled at Jake and Ross. 'Bushmeat?' he enquired, confirming Jake's worst suspicions.

'Er, no thanks,' Jake stammered, turning away quickly and bumping into a burly man behind him. 'Sorry,' he said, stepping to one side.

But the man hardly noticed Jake. He seemed more interested in the meat and began a lively discussion in Swahili with the trader. Jake and Ross hurried away, but before they were out of earshot, Jake overheard bits of the conversation. He understood the words meaning *more money*, *too much*, and *good meat*, and he guessed that the two men were haggling over the price.

'I just hope that isn't chimp meat,' Jake said miserably, taking a last glance back at the stall. The merchant was counting out a thick bundle of notes while the customer looked on.

'Hard to tell,' said Ross. 'It's been smoked and could be anything really – crocodile, bush pig, monkey . . .' He paused then added with a wicked grin, 'human.'

'Oh, rubbish,' Jake laughed.

Ross turned into a dead-end alley. 'We can get the batteries from a shop down here,' he said.

Jake shifted the bag of bananas to his other shoulder and followed Ross down the narrow road. Unlike the main street, there were no market stalls here, just a few small shops. On the wall of one was a hand-painted sign. *DAKTARI*, read the thick black letters while beneath it was another, smaller sign saying, *'Dr. T. K. Mbozo. M.D. Kampala. Treatment of all sicknesses. Spells removed. Love problems solved.'*

'Sounds like an amazing doctor,' Jake whistled.

'He is,' agreed Ross. 'He cured me once.'

'From a spell?' Jake teased.

'Yes,' said Ross, poker-faced.

'You're kidding!' Jake said, and Ross, unable to keep a straight face any longer, replied laughingly, 'A spell of malaria!'

The battery shop was next-door to the doctor's rooms. Jake and Ross were about to enter when a loud shriek sounded from further down the road. The painfully familiar sound made Jake feel as if a cold hand was clamped round his throat. 'Chimps!' he exclaimed.

Ross nodded. 'Behind that lorry,' he said. He pointed to a tall-sided truck parked near the end of the alley, and set off at a trot to investigate.

Jake ran after him, only too aware now of more chimp noises – distressed whimpers and squeaks that spoke of fear and misery.

At the back of the lorry, the two swing doors were wide open. A plaintive cry of *hoo*, *hoo*, *hoo* spilled out from the gloomy interior.

Jake peered inside. A couple of wooden crates were stacked up at one side. He craned his neck, trying to spot the chimp he knew must be hidden somewhere in there. Then he saw a tiny black hand sticking out from one of the crates. Without thinking, Jake hoisted himself up into the lorry.

'Careful,' warned Ross. 'Someone might come.'

But Jake's only concern at that moment was for

the infant in the crate. Slipping the bag of bananas off his shoulder, he crept over to the chimpanzee. He'd just reached it when Ross called out in a hoarse whisper, 'Hide! Someone's coming.'

Frantically, Jake looked around. There was a narrow gap between the side of the lorry and the crates. He squeezed behind the crates, flattening himself against the lorry wall. Somewhere a door slammed, then heavy footsteps sounded outside. Next came the sound of someone grunting as if a heavy object was being lifted. Jake peeped out to see another crate being pushed into the lorry. A man glanced briefly inside before going away again.

Jake waited, listening to the man's footsteps fading down the pavement. A tiny whimpering came from the new crate. *Another baby!* Jake realized with dismay. He could guess what was going on here. These chimps were going to be sold as pets!

With the coast apparently clear, Jake eased himself out of his hiding place and crept over to the first crate. It was made from panels of wood which were solid except for a few holes drilled haphazardly here and there. Most of the holes were quite small – airholes, Jake assumed. But some were big enough for a chimp's hand to reach through. The little black hand had disappeared but as Jake peered in through one of the larger holes he saw the hand reaching towards him from the shadows. Gentle leathery fingers patted his face, while from inside came a woeful *hoo, hoo, hoo.*

Jake touched the chimp's hand and the little fingers curled round his thumb. 'Don't worry, we're going to rescue you,' Jake whispered, even though he hadn't a clue how right then. A small movement outside the door made Jake freeze.

But it was only Ross. He climbed inside. 'This is way too dangerous,' he whispered. 'We've got to get out of here.'

There was a burst of cheerful whistling outside. Someone was heading for the lorry.

'Hide!' hissed Ross, tucking himself behind the crate that had just been loaded.

There was no time for Jake to scuttle back to his gap. A shape appeared in the doorway, blocking out the light. Jake dropped to the floor and lay flat on his stomach, not daring to breathe. There was a jolt and a thud, then silence. Slowly, Jake looked up. Daylight was coming in through the door again. There was a fourth crate in the lorry, this one bigger than the others. It had a small barred window in one side.

Jake and Ross crawled over to it. A tiny rustling noise came from inside and then, as Jake looked in, a little pink face appeared at the window. It was a very young chimpanzee.

Ross whistled quietly. 'Poor thing. It's way too young to be away from its mother. It can't be more than about a month old.'

The baby chimp stared at them, dazed and frightened. It whimpered, then lifted one tiny hand and pushed it through the bars. There was an ugly wound on the baby's wrist, edged with black scorch marks.

'It's been shot!' Jake gasped. He peered into the crate and saw that the baby wasn't alone. There were at least two others shut in there with it. And from what Jake could make out in the gloom, one of them looked in a very bad way. 'There's a really tiny one in here curled up in a heap,' he told Ross.

Ross looked grim. 'I'm going for help,' he said. 'You wait—'

Voices were coming their way, terrifyingly near. There was no chance to get out, or even hide.

We're done for, thought Jake, a shiver of fear running through him. People who dealt in the illegal chimp trade were hardly likely to welcome him and Ross on board their lorry. He pushed himself against the crate, trying to melt into the background. Something creaked outside and there was a loud slam followed by darkness. The doors had been closed.

'They're about to drive away!' Jake croaked hoarsely.

'Quick! Let's get out of here,' said Ross.

Expecting the engines to start up at any moment, Jake clambered to the back of the lorry. In the dark, he and Ross fumbled about, trying to find a way to open the doors. 'I've found the bolt,' Jake said, his hand grasping an upright metal rod. He tried to slide it up, but nothing happened. 'They must have locked the door from the outside,' he said.

Desperately, he knelt down and jerked at the end of the rod where it met the floor. Ross grabbed it higher up and yanked hard too. It shot up with a *clunk*, pinching Jake's fingers painfully. Behind him, one of the chimps let out a loud shriek.

Jake flinched. What if the driver came to investigate?

Holding their breath, Jake and Ross waited, ready to hide the moment they heard someone coming. The chimpanzee shrieked again. Another one began to whimper, then a third joined in.

'Ssh,' Jake urged, crawling over to the crate that contained the tiniest babies. He felt around until he found the bars and slipped his hand through. Agile fingers curled around his, while another hand poked through the bars, and, finding Jake's face, clung on desperately to his chin.

Ross opened the doors a crack and peeped outside.

'There's no one there,' he whispered. 'Come on. Let's go.'

Jake gently unfurled the little fingers from his chin. 'We'll come back for you,' he promised. He crept over to the door and slipped out of the lorry behind Ross.

'Now what?' Jake asked, as they quietly swung the doors shut. He wondered why the lorry hadn't driven off yet. They stole round to the side of the vehicle, keeping a lookout for anyone who might be coming.

Jake peered at the cab, trying to see if anyone was in there. 'Watch out!' he hissed, as the driver's door was flung open and a man jumped down to the ground.

'In here,' said Ross, grabbing Jake's arm.

They ducked into a doorway, pretending to read a notice pinned to the door as the man walked past. Jake sneaked a look at him and frowned. He'd seen the burly figure before. It was the customer from the bushmeat stall.

Ross craned his neck and watched the man disappear. 'You stay here and keep watch,' he said. 'I'm going for the cops.'

'What if he drives off before you get back?' Jake asked.

'Then stop him!' Ross darted out from the doorway and sprinted back up the alley to the main street.

Stop him! thought Jake, shaking his head. *I wish I could.* He stepped out from the doorway and, with his hands in his pockets, glanced up and down the road, trying to look casual. He wondered where the driver had gone. *Only one way to find out*, he decided. Steeling himself, and feeling anything but brave, he headed back down the alley.

It looked like the man had gone down a narrow driveway that led to a garage. Through the doors, Jake could see a battered open-backed Land Rover. On the back of the four-wheel drive was a rickety-looking wire cage.

I wonder if the chimps were brought here in that? Jake asked himself. Making sure that no one was about, he sprinted down the driveway and slipped into the garage. He climbed on to the back bumper of the Land Rover to get a good look at the cage. A thin layer of straw and leaves covered the floor and several tufts of black hair were caught in the wire mesh. *Chimp hair!* Jake thought, fingering one of the tufts.

He jumped down silently then slipped round to the front and climbed on to the running-board below the door. Gripping the door handle to keep himself steady, he looked in through the open window.

Empty drink cans littered the floor and bits of stuffing bulged out from the worn seats. Jake was about to get down again when he noticed something long and thin sticking out from behind the seat, just next to the driver's door. The strange-looking object was wrapped in a distinctively patterned red and white cloth. Jake's heart began to thud. It was just like the cloth that had covered the severed chimpanzee hands and feet in the forest!

EIGHT

'Isaac! Hurry up. You're making us late.'

The man's voice was close – too close for comfort. Jake hopped down, ready to run, but there was no time. A door was creaking open in the corner of the garage. Jake dropped to the ground and dived under the Land Rover, praying he hadn't been seen.

'Sorry,' a second man muttered as the door slammed shut. 'I was just getting food for the journey.'

Jake felt a wave of relief. They hadn't spotted him. Lying flat on the grimy floor, he peered out from under the vehicle. Two pairs of dusty boots clumped towards him and stopped less than a hand's length away. Jake went cold. What if they were about to drive the Land Rover away?

'We need to take this too,' said the first man.

Jake heard the driver's door swing open. Someone reached inside and pulled something out, then the door was banged shut again. Specks of dust floated down on to Jake's head, and he screwed up his nose to stop himself sneezing.

'OK. Let's go,' said the second man.

Jake heard the men tramping away, their footsteps growing fainter. When he couldn't hear them any longer, he dragged himself across the grease-covered floor to the back of the vehicle and looked up the driveway. The two figures were about to turn into the alley. They were carrying what looked like bags of food as well as the cloth parcel Jake had seen in the Land Rover.

Jake waited until they'd turned the corner then crawled out from under the vehicle. Keeping low, he darted up the drive. As he reached the top, he heard the men talking earnestly just metres away. They sounded worked up, as if they were in some kind of trouble. Jake flattened himself against the wall and peeped round the corner.

The back of the lorry was wide open and the men were staring at it in consternation. Their bags and the cloth parcel were dumped in a heap at their feet. 'I tell you, someone's been here,' said the burly man, glancing round suspiciously.

Jake shrank back against the wall. *We should have shut the doors*, he realized with a jolt of dread. If the men spotted him, they would probably put two and two together and work out that he knew about their illegal cargo. What would that mean for the baby chimps? Would the men destroy them to get rid of the evidence? Jake held his breath and peered round the corner again, straining to hear the rest of the conversation.

'*Siyo, ndugu*,' responded the other man. 'No one's been here. We just didn't shut the doors properly. They swung open on their own. It always happens.' He went to close them but his brother grabbed his arm and stopped him.

'You say no one's been here, Isaac,' he said, heaving himself into the back of the lorry. 'So what's this, then?' He went inside and reappeared a moment later with a canvas bag which he dropped on the ground in front of Isaac. It was the bag of bananas!

Jake's mouth felt dry. *You idiot!* he cursed himself.

The big man leaped down from the lorry and angrily banged the doors shut.

'It's just bananas, Moses,' Isaac said to him, checking inside the bag. 'Someone left them for the chimpanzees.'

'*Juha!*' snapped Moses, edgily. 'Don't be such a fool. Who would do that?'

'Young boys coming to play with the chimps?' suggested Isaac.

'Why would young—' Moses began, then he

stopped, his jaw dropping as something came to him. 'It *was* young guys,' he growled. 'I saw them at the *nyama* stall. One of them was carrying this!' He kicked at the bag at Isaac's feet. 'We have to go,' he said urgently. 'Those two *kijanas* are on to us. They must have tracked us down from Luama.'

Luama! The word echoed in the empty alley, sounding loudly in Jake's head. Moses had just admitted that he and Isaac had come from the chimp sanctuary! These men had to be the poachers that had ambushed the A-community. And the infants in the crates at the back of the lorry must be the last of Ashai's family.

Jake felt desperate. *Ross is right. I've got to stop them*, he thought. And then came a stroke of incredible good luck. A noisy truck came lurching down the alley and parked just in front of the poachers' lorry, blocking its exit.

'Hey! We have to leave,' shouted Moses, waving his arms frantically at the truck.

The driver turned off the engine and leaned out of his window. 'What's the problem?' he called.

'You've blocked us in,' Moses yelled.

'You must wait five minutes,' responded the driver calmly, opening his door and jumping down. 'I have medicine for the *daktari*.'

Moses frowned. 'We have urgent business,' he

said, striding towards the newcomer. 'And you're holding us up.'

'What urgent business?' asked the driver, his hands on his hips.

A loud shriek sounded from the hunters' lorry. The truck driver frowned.

'Parrots,' said Isaac hastily. 'For the president. We have to take them to Kampala.'

If he believes that, he'll believe anything, thought Jake, hoping the newcomer would be suspicious and at least ask to see the parrots.

But to Jake's disappointment, the man didn't seem sceptical at all. 'The parrots and the president will have to be patient for a few minutes longer,' he said, walking round to the back of his truck.

'Let's help him. Then he'll go sooner,' Isaac suggested, shrugging at his companion.

Leaving their own bags by the back door of the lorry, they went to the back of the truck and started to unload a stack of cardboard boxes which they carried one by one into the doctor's building.

Gingerly, Jake stepped out and looked up the alley. *Come on, Ross*, he begged silently. But there was no sign of Ross or the police. Jake clenched his fists in frustration. In a few minutes, the poachers would be gone and the chimps would be on their way to a dismal life of captivity.

Jake felt helpless. Then his eyes fell on the red and white cloth parcel that was leaning against one of the food bags behind the lorry. Perhaps this was something that would link the men to the massacre in the Luama forest.

Jake raced over, grabbed the parcel, then ducked behind an overflowing rubbish skip on the other side of the alley. He was only just in time. Moses and Isaac came out from the Daktari's rooms and strode back to their lorry. They tossed the food bags, including the one with the bananas, into the back then slammed the doors and hurried round to the cab.

Phew! thought Jake. *Just as well they're in such a hurry. They didn't even notice this was missing!* He clutched the object in his hands and sneaked a look round the rubbish skip at the vehicles. He saw the truck reversing up the alley, then the lorry began to pull away too. With its engine roaring and black smoke belching out of the exhaust, the chimp transporter moved slowly towards the main street. And there was nothing Jake could do to stop it.

He stood up and slammed his fist into the side of the skip. 'Blast!' he cursed through clenched teeth. He startled a stork which had been picking in the rubbish. It clattered its bill loudly and jumped down to the ground. With its head lowered, it ran along the pavement then took off and soared away in the same direction as the lorry.

'I could do with a pair of wings too,' Jake muttered. Tucking the parcel under his arm, he started up the alley after the lorry, keeping in the shadows beside the buildings.

The vehicle turned the corner into the busy road and Jake lost sight of it. He lengthened his stride and emerged from the alley in time to see the lorry lurch to a stop only metres ahead of him as a cyclist veered in front of it. The jolt made the back doors swing open.

Jake saw the big crate sliding across the floor inside. It bumped to a halt against the door frame, its small barred window facing out on to the street. As Moses put his foot down, the lorry shot forward and the doors slammed shut again.

But in the brief moment that he'd seen inside, Jake locked eyes with one of the infants in the crate. The little chimpanzee had stared straight at him in a silent cry for help, reaching pitifully through the bars with its wounded hand.

NINE

In a last effort to do something that might help save the baby chimps, Jake memorized the lorry's number plate. 'KL 4937,' he repeated over and over again as he darted through the crowds, trying to keep up with the vehicle. For a while, the crowds were on his side and it looked as if he was going to catch up. He thought wildly about trying to grab on to the side of the lorry, but just then a rare break in the traffic gave Moses the chance to speed up. Within minutes, the lorry had merged with the rest of the traffic and disappeared from sight.

Defeated, Jake slumped against a wall, breathing hard. 'So that's that,' he said miserably. He sank down and rested the cloth-wrapped parcel on his knees. 'This probably won't mean a thing now that they've got away,' he muttered, fingering the red and white material. For the first time since he'd snatched the wrapped-up object, he had time to wonder what it was.

A grubby piece of string was tied round it. Jake unwound it and the cloth fell open on his lap to reveal a sleek black rifle. 'Oh wow!' he gasped. It was just like the ones his stepdad, Rick, and the rangers at Musabi carried when they were out in the bush.

But there was one big difference. Rick and his men hardly ever pulled the triggers on their guns. They carried them purely for self-defence.

Jake shuddered. He wasn't allowed to go anywhere near Rick's rifle, let alone handle it. When the guns weren't being used, Rick kept them locked up in a special strongroom. Yet here Jake was, holding a rifle in full view of everyone in Baguru, and it was probably loaded, too! With his heart pounding, Jake came to his senses and covered the gun with the cloth. Luckily, the passers-by seemed too absorbed in their own business to notice him crouching against the wall with the rifle.

Making sure it was pointing downwards, Jake stood up. Feeling ultra-conspicuous, he went to stand next to the road, looking up and down to see if the Luama jeep was coming yet. Eventually he spotted it in the distance. Walking as fast as he dared through a crowded market with a loaded gun in one hand, Jake went to meet the jeep.

It pulled up next to him and Jake saw that his

mother was driving. Ross was in the front seat next to her. 'Hi. Where's your mum?' Jake asked Ross.

'Behind us, with Sergeant Lubumba,' said Ross, pointing over his shoulder.

Jake saw a beige-coloured Land Rover pull up behind the jeep. A tall uniformed man stepped out. Liz followed him.

'Where are the *mwindajis*?' the policeman asked Jake.

'Gone,' he replied. He pointed in the direction the poachers had gone. 'About fifteen minutes ago. I bet we could catch them up, though,' he added, hopefully.

'Did you get their number plate?' asked the sergeant.

Jake nodded. 'KL 493. Er, 9. I mean, 7,' he said. 'And I got this, too.' He handed over the rifle.

Sergeant Lubumba pulled off the cloth, exposing the gleaming gun.

'Jake!' exclaimed Hannah from the jeep. 'You know you're not supposed to handle guns.'

'I know,' Jake said. 'But I just took it because of the cloth. It's the same as the one we found in the forest. I didn't realize it was a gun until I unwrapped it. Honest!'

Ross looked at Jake with respect. 'How did you get it?'

'I just grabbed it when the men weren't looking,' Jake explained.

The policeman pulled back the bolt and shook the bullets out into his hand.

'It's loaded!' gasped Hannah. 'There could have been a terrible accident.'

'But there wasn't,' Jake argued. 'And I had to get some proof. You see, I think they're the same people who shot the A-community the other night. I heard them talking about Luama.'

'Even if they're not the ones, we've got to go after them,' said Liz urgently. 'Sergeant, those chimps must be rescued before they reach the border.'

'Right. Let's go then,' said Sergeant Lubumba, shouldering the rifle and striding back to the Land Rover.

'I'll go with the sergeant in case we get separated,' Liz said to the others. 'If he catches up with the poachers, he'll have a job to deal with the chimps on his own.' She hurried back to the Land Rover.

'I hope we don't get separated,' Jake said, climbing into the front of the jeep alongside his mum and Ross. Seeing as he and Ross had been the ones to find the poachers, he wanted to be in on all the action.

Hannah waited for the Land Rover to pull out first, then she edged her way behind it into the clogged-up road.

Like the rest of the traffic in the street, the two vehicles made very slow progress. Jake's stomach knotted up in frustration. With every passing moment, Isaac and Moses were speeding further away from them. 'Why doesn't Sergeant Lubumba make all the traffic give way?' Jake said with an impatient sigh.

Almost as if he'd heard Jake, the sergeant switched on a siren. The lorries and taxis parted at once, leaving the way clear for the jeep and Land Rover.

'That's unusual,' said Ross, as Hannah accelerated. 'Normally no one takes any notice of police sirens.'

'It must be our lucky day,' Hannah said grimly, keeping her eyes fixed on the road.

They shot down the main street, past astonished shoppers who leaped out of their way then stood gaping after them. Within minutes they had reached the outskirts of Baguru and were hurtling along a dirt road past shanty houses standing in small patches of maize and other crops.

'Watch out! Pothole!' yelled Ross, grabbing the dashboard.

Hannah swerved just in time to avoid a muddy hole in the middle of the road. 'Thanks,' she said.

They sped on, dodging more potholes, some of them more like craters. Hannah also had to keep giving way to cattle, donkeys and goats that hopped out in front of them, then ambled slowly across the road.

Each time they stopped, Jake's anxiety reached a new pitch. 'Can't you go faster, Mum?' he urged her.

'I'm driving as fast as I can,' Hannah told him sternly. 'Unless you'd rather we end up like that.' She pointed to the rusting remains of a car that had overturned in a deep ditch at the side of the road.

'OK, OK,' Jake muttered. He tried to stay calm, but when they turned off the dirt track and on to a wider tarred road, he noticed the police vehicle slipping further away from them. 'Look, we're losing them,' he said.

They rounded a sharp corner and found themselves at the foot of a long, steep hill. The police Land Rover was already about halfway up but it was going at a snail's pace behind a queue of cars, trucks and taxis. Ahead, holding up all the traffic, was a huge lorry heavily laden with logs.

'Oh, no!' Jake groaned, drumming the dashboard with his fingers. 'Just our luck to get caught behind this lot.'

'I know a short cut,' said Ross. 'It's rough, but it'll save us lots of time.'

Hannah frowned. 'How rough?'

'Er, very,' replied Ross. He pointed to a tree at the side of the road. 'It's just past that tree. Not a lot of people go that way. But Dad and I always use it.' He grinned at Jake. 'It's great for practising off-road driving.'

'You mean your dad lets you drive there?' Jake asked him, catching his drift.

'Yep!' smiled Ross. 'If you can drive on a road like that, you can drive anywhere!'

'Well, I'll give it a go,' said Hannah, gripping the steering wheel and wrenching it round so that they slewed off the road.

Jake quickly found out what Ross was talking about. The short cut was little more than a twisting, rutted path cut through thick bush. In places it rose steeply up muddy embankments then dropped down sharply on the other side.

'You weren't exaggerating,' said Hannah, as they bounced and skidded down a slippery bank.

'Don't worry,' Ross told her. 'It's not like this all the way.'

At the bottom of the bank, the Land Rover ground to a halt in a deep, muddy ditch. Hannah pressed her foot gently on the accelerator but the wheels just spun uselessly.

Jake held his breath. It looked like they were stuck!

'Use the diff lock,' said Ross, pointing to a switch on the dashboard. 'Then all the wheels will move together.'

'Great, I was hoping there was one of those,' said Hannah. She flicked the switch then shifted into first gear. Gently she let out the clutch and the jeep rocked forward a little way before stopping again.

Jake groaned. 'Great short cut,' he muttered as Hannah pushed down the clutch so that the jeep rocked backwards once more. 'We'll be here all day.'

Hannah shot him a sideways glance. 'Trust me. I know what I'm doing,' she said.

By making it rock back and forth a few more times, Hannah gradually coaxed the jeep out of the ditch and on to more solid ground.

'Brilliant driving, Mum!' Jake breathed out with relief.

'That was the worst part,' Ross reassured them once they were on their way again.

A few minutes later the track rejoined the main road. 'We're on the other side of that steep hill now,' Ross explained.

Jake looked back and saw the log transporter just appearing at the top of the hill. Cars and taxis began to overtake the lorry, but there was no sign of the beige Land Rover.

'They must still be coming up the hill,' Jake said.

'Well, we'll keep going. I'm sure they'll catch us up soon enough,' said Hannah, putting her foot down.

The road stretched straight ahead. They shot past a sign reading, *Port Bell. 15 km.*

'So that's where they're going,' Jake said.

'Yeah. They'll probably take the ferry across Lake Victoria then drive to Dar es Salaam or Mombasa on the Kenyan coast,' said Ross.

'And then?' Jake asked.

'The chimps will be loaded on to ships and sent to dealers in other countries,' answered Ross quietly.

'Not this time,' Jake vowed. But he couldn't help feeling that with only fifteen kilometres to Port Bell, they were probably already too late. He stared ahead. In front of them, a lorry was parked next to the road. Jake saw that the hood was raised. 'Looks like it's broken down,' Jake remarked but as they got closer, he suddenly realized he'd seen the lorry before. 'Stop!' he yelled out to his mum. 'That's them! The poachers!'

Hannah braked and came to a stop quite a way behind the lorry. Jake grabbed the door handle and was about to leap out when Hannah grabbed his arm. 'Hang on, Jake. No heroics now. We'll leave this to the sergeant.'

'But what if the poachers get going again?' Jake pleaded. 'Or see us and run away?'

'It's a risk we'll have to take,' said Hannah. 'We can't confront them. I don't even like being parked so close to them. Who knows how many other guns they're carrying?'

It seemed hours before Sergeant Lubumba's Land Rover drew up alongside them. 'What's up?' asked Liz through her window.

'The poachers,' Ross announced briefly, pointing to the lorry.

'This is very good luck,' said Sergeant Lubumba, baring his teeth in a grin as he leaned across from the driving seat. 'But not for the *mwindajis*.' He parked the Land Rover in front of the jeep then stepped out on to the road. 'Wait here, everyone,' he said. Adjusting the revolver on his hip, he strode towards the lorry.

Jake stared out of the front window, his heart racing. 'Do you think Moses and Isaac will put up a fight?' he asked Ross.

'Probably,' said Ross. 'Those chimps are worth a lot of money to them.'

'They'd better not hurt them,' Jake said, picturing a gun battle with bullets ricocheting off the crates.

But there was no sudden burst of gunfire, just silence as the sergeant strolled confidently down the side of the lorry then disappeared round the front.

Jake couldn't stand the suspense. 'Can't we go and see what's happening?' he asked his mum.

'Not yet,' she answered.

For a few minutes, nothing happened. Even the road was quiet now that the traffic that had been caught behind the lorry had gone past.

Suddenly a tall figure appeared and went round to the back of the lorry. 'That's Isaac,' Jake whispered. 'He must be going to open the back for the sergeant.'

Next came Moses. He was handcuffed to Sergeant Lubumba, arguing loudly.

Jake leaned out of his window, hoping to hear what the men were saying.

'If it's just bananas in there, then why won't you let me look inside?' asked the policeman.

'Because . . . well . . . you see, there's er . . . livestock in there too and they might escape and go running all over the road,' argued Moses, trying to step in front of the policeman.

But the policeman ignored him and simply walked on with Moses shuffling along reluctantly at his side. 'Open up, Kumalo!' the sergeant ordered Isaac who was leaning against the doors.

'I can't,' said Isaac weakly. 'My brother and I, we lost the key.'

'Lost the key!' Jake echoed scornfully. 'Liar! There isn't one.'

Hearing Jake, Isaac looked straight at him. The poacher's jaw dropped and his eyes grew wide. He looked as if he'd seen a ghost. *'Kijanas!'* he gasped.

'You were right, Moses. The young guys from Luama found us.'

'I told you!' Moses spat back, glaring at Jake and Ross.

The policeman pushed Isaac to one side and reached up with his free hand to open the doors.

'No!' yelled Moses, trying to knock away the policeman's hand. 'You mustn't. The animals . . .'

The doors swung open, revealing the cargo of wooden crates. A volley of frightened shrieks broke out from inside the lorry. Jake couldn't stand it any longer. He pushed open his door, jumped to the ground and sprinted to the lorry. Almost bowling Isaac over, he scrambled inside.

Behind him, Hannah shouted out, 'Jake! Stop!' But her words were lost in the barrage of screams and whimpers that filled Jake's ears.

'It's OK. It's OK,' he soothed, pushing his hand through the windows of the biggest crate. 'You're safe now.' He looked for a way of opening the box and saw a heavy padlock. 'Where's the key?' he demanded, looking over his shoulder at the astonished Isaac.

The poacher took a step backwards, almost standing on the policeman's foot.

'You heard him,' ordered the policeman, quickly handcuffing Isaac to the other man.

Isaac rifled in his pocket then, glowering at Jake, tossed him a key.

'Thanks,' said Jake, catching it. He turned the key in the padlock and started easing the lid of the crate open just as Hannah, Ross and Liz appeared at the door.

'Hold on,' said Ross, hauling himself up. 'I'll give you a hand.'

Together, Jake and Ross pulled up the lid. Daylight flooded into the crate and fell on not three, but five baby chimpanzees. They sat huddled together in one corner, hardly moving, their eyes sunken into their heads and their faces frozen into expressions of sheer terror.

'You're safe. You're safe,' Jake repeated. Slowly he stretched his hand towards the infants. One of them blinked and, whimpering softly, reached out to touch the tips of Jake's fingers. The delicate touch seemed filled with gratitude and trust, as if the chimp understood that not all humans were bad. Jake looked down at the little hand. It was the chimp with the gunshot wound on its wrist.

TEN

'We need to get them back to Luama as fast as we can,' said Liz, appearing in the lorry beside Jake. She reached into the crate and picked up the tiniest baby. It clung limply to her, its eyes half-closed. 'This one's in a really bad way.'

'Will they be all right?' Jake asked anxiously. He and Ross had started to open the crates containing the other two chimps.

'I hope so,' sighed Liz. 'But I can't promise anything.' She came over and looked at the two chimpanzees cowering miserably in their small boxes. 'These are slightly older so they might fare better,' she said. 'But right now they're in shock, and it looks like they're all badly dehydrated.'

'What? You mean they've been given nothing to drink?' asked Hannah. She'd also climbed into the lorry and was taking photographs of the traumatized infants.

'Or eat, most likely,' said Liz.

This made no sense to Jake. 'But if the chimps are so valuable, how come the hunters don't look after them properly?' he protested, smoothing the head of the infant clinging to Liz.

'Good question,' said Liz. 'Either they don't know how to look after them, or they don't care.'

'Probably a bit of both,' put in Ross. He tried to pick up one of the older chimps but it shrank fearfully away from him.

'I guess the poor little soul doesn't trust humans right now,' murmured Hannah as she took a picture of the frightened baby.

Meanwhile, Sergeant Lubumba had handcuffed the Kumalo brothers inside the Land Rover so that he could have a good look at the lorry and its precious cargo. 'There's enough evidence here to put those men in prison for a long time,' he said, reappearing at the back with two pangas, another rifle and several boxes of bullets.

Jake swallowed. Obviously there was no shortage of weapons in the poaching operation.

'They must be doing well if they can afford that much ammo,' Ross remarked.

'Well, they should have spent some of their profits on maintaining their lorry,' said Sergeant Lubumba.

'What's wrong with it?' Jake asked.

'Head gasket's blown, I think,' answered the sergeant.

Ross whistled. 'That means a tow truck will have to come from Port Bell to collect it.'

'But what about the chimps?' Jake protested. 'They can't stay here until the lorry gets towed away.'

'Absolutely,' agreed Liz. 'We'll have to transfer them to the jeep.'

'But the crates won't fit in the jeep,' Ross pointed out.

'We're not taking the crates,' replied his mum. 'Just the chimps. We'll hold them on our laps.' She turned to Hannah. 'Would you mind driving again? This little one's not going to want to let go of me for a while.' She glanced down at the frail baby in her arms. 'I'm afraid it's going to be touch and go for her. We have a few basic medical supplies at Luama, but she's going to need more than we can provide.'

While Jake and Ross kept an eye on the chimps, Hannah reversed the jeep close to the back of the lorry.

'Put the others on the back seat with me,' said Liz, climbing inside with the baby.

Jake, Ross and Hannah carefully lifted the chimps out of their crates and transferred them to the jeep. The trembling babies seemed resigned to their fate because they put up no resistance, apart from a few anxious grunts and whimpers.

The last one to be taken out was the infant with the bullet wound. 'Your turn,' Jake said, reaching into the crate. The little chimp scrambled to his feet and eagerly stretched up his arms, allowing Jake to pick him up. 'I wonder if you were playing with Ashai a few days ago,' Jake mused sadly as the baby snuggled close to him. He stared over his shoulder at the two poachers in the Land Rover. What incredible misery they had caused for those beautiful creatures.

Holding the baby safely on his hip, Jake clambered down from the lorry. 'That's it,' he said to Sergeant Lubumba who nodded and slammed the lorry doors shut before walking back to his Land Rover.

'Thank you for helping me catch these men,' he called to Jake and Ross before driving away. 'They're big fish, the Kumalos. We've been trying to catch them for a long time now.'

'Terrific!' Jake exclaimed, watching the Land Rover do a U-turn in the road and head back up the hill towards Baguru. He exchanged a triumphant grin with Ross. 'Now the forests will be a lot safer for the chimps.'

They arrived back at Luama late that afternoon. Jake had expected the trip to be difficult with seven young chimps loose inside the jeep, but the traumatized infants hardly moved. Jake sat on the front seat with the injured male on his lap. The little chimp gripped Jake's arms tightly at first but eventually he relaxed and fell asleep for the rest of the journey.

'Do you think Ashai will recognize them?' Jake asked Ross when they pulled up at the sanctuary.

'Oh sure,' said Ross. 'As long as they're all from the same community.'

'You mean some of these might not be from Ashai's group?' Jake asked, surprised.

'I'd say about half aren't,' Ross told him. 'I don't think the A-community had as many babies as this. But Dad will know.'

David came over from the tents, looking very puzzled. 'Where have you been all day?' he asked. 'I was getting really worried about—' He stopped abruptly. 'Well, strike me down!' he exclaimed, staring in disbelief at the seven subdued chimpanzees in the jeep. 'Where did you find this lot?'

'On the way to Port Bell with the Kumalo brothers,' said Liz. 'We'll tell you all about it later. Right now, these chimps need a lot of attention.'

They carried the orphans into the treatment hut near Ashai's enclosure and settled most of them in an airy straw-lined cage while Liz set up a drip for the frail infant in her arms. But one chimp refused to go in with the others – the male that Jake had held in the jeep. The minute he saw the bars on the cage, he screamed in protest and clung tightly to Jake.

'Not again,' Jake sighed, wondering what he had done to turn himself into chimp velcro.

'Well, how would you feel about being put in another cage if you were that chimp?' asked Hannah, taking a picture of the orphans curled up together in the straw.

'I suppose I'd be dead scared,' Jake admitted.

'He'll be OK when he sees the others eating,' said David. He turned to Ross. 'Could you fetch some avocados and bananas from the kitchen please, Ross?'

'I'll help you,' offered Hannah, going out with Ross.

With Jake still holding the little male, David examined the wound on the infant's wrist. 'Mmm. Looks nasty. I think we'd better give him a shot of antibiotics,' he said. He took a syringe and a phial of medicine out of a steel trunk.

'It looks like a bullet injury, like the one on Ashai's shoulder,' Jake suggested as David gently pushed the needle into the chimp's hairy arm.

'Yes, I think you're right,' said David, his eyes dark with anger.

The chimp gave a loud shriek and jerked his arm away just as David finished injecting him. He glared at David. Wrinkling his brow in a deep frown, he peered at the spot where the needle had gone in and sulkily patted his fur.

'With that kind of spirit, I reckon you'll be just fine,' smiled David, taking the chimp from Jake and giving him a cuddle. 'There, you've forgiven me now, haven't you?' he chuckled as the chimp snuggled against his neck.

'What about this one?' asked Liz, still cradling the frail baby. A plastic tube led from the infant's arm to a bag of fluid that she was trying to hook up on a nail in the wall. She glanced at Jake. 'Hold her for me for a minute, please,' she asked him. 'I need to get this fixed up.'

Jake took the baby from Liz and held her in the crook of his arm. The tiny infant was as light as a bird. She lay very still, her eyes closed and her breaths coming in short, shallow puffs so that her bony rib-cage barely rose as she breathed. Jake looked at the thin plastic tube that was carrying fluid into her veins. *How long before this starts working?* he wondered.

'I think I should radio the vet in Kampala, don't you?' said Liz, when the bag of fluid was in place.

David was dabbing some ointment on to the baby

male's wrist. He carried him over to look at the sickly infant. 'I don't think the vet would get here in time,' he said, quietly.

Jake jerked his head up. This was the last thing he had expected to hear. He'd assumed that with careful handling, the baby would eventually recover, just like Ashai. 'Won't the drip make her stronger?' he asked.

David looked at him, his brown eyes troubled. 'Probably not,' he said. 'She's in deep shock. And a bit too far down the road for us to bring her out of it.'

'All the same, I'll see if I can get a message to Dr Nyandwi,' said Liz, going to the door. But before she could leave, the injured chimp in David's arms began hooting softly. 'What's the matter, little one?' Liz asked, turning back.

The chimp was staring at the tiny baby held by Jake. He frowned then hooted more loudly, stretching out one hand to stroke the baby's smooth pink cheek.

Jake saw her eyelids flutter and he felt her take a deeper breath. The male hooted again, then leaned forward and pressed his lips against the baby's face, as if he was kissing her. The sick infant gave the faintest of whimpers before breathing out with a hushed sigh.

Jake waited for her to take another breath. But the limp body in his arms was quite still. *Breathe*, Jake urged silently. The older chimp picked up one of the baby's dangling arms and shook it rather roughly.

'It's too late,' David said gently, prising the chimp's hand away from the baby's arm. 'There's nothing anyone can do for her now.'

Jake swallowed hard and blinked back sudden hot tears. He stared down at the lifeless body. 'I wish we'd found you earlier,' he whispered hoarsely. 'And I wish people would leave the chimps alone.' He felt a tide of anger rising within him, so that he wanted to slam his fist into the wall. 'It's such a waste,' he protested as Liz came over and put an arm round his shoulders.

'We all did our best,' she said kindly. 'Especially you.'

Jake bit his lip. The chimpanzee's tiny body was still warm in his arms. Jake thought about the first community of chimps they'd seen the other day. One of the babies had been about the same size as this little one, clinging safely to its mother's tummy as she padded away into the forest. 'And that's how you should be too,' Jake said to the dead infant. 'Not like this.' He swallowed again. 'But at least you didn't die in that horrible crate on the back of a lorry.'

Liz slid her hands under the tiny body and lifted it out of Jake's arms. 'We'll lay her to rest near the lake, beside the others we've lost over the years.'

She was about to go through the door when Hannah and Ross came back carrying two bowls of fruit. 'Oh, no!' cried Hannah, seeing the dead chimp. She put her dish down then rested one hand on the baby's wrinkled forehead. 'I'm so sorry that humans did this to you,' she murmured, tears welling up in her eyes. She paused, then traced a finger around the closed eyes and the silent mouth. 'But we'll always remember you,' she promised. 'And I'll make sure that thousands of other humans hear all about what you went through.' Fumbling blindly for her camera, she raised it and focussed on the little face. The shutter clicked, snapping loudly in the silent hut.

Ross and the Kirbys looked on silently while Hannah took a few more photographs. Sitting on David's hip, the young male chimp also gazed miserably at the dead infant. He whimpered and stretched across to grab the body from Liz. David stepped quickly away, soothing the unhappy chimp with his free hand.

'He's really cut up,' Jake said to Ross.

Ross nodded. 'We've often seen chimps go into mourning when a family member dies. They kind of stare into space and look miserable for ages.'

A loud rumbling in the air signalled that a thunderstorm was on its way. David handed the male chimp back to Jake and eased the tiny body from Liz's hands. 'You all stay here and see the chimps get enough to eat while I bury her,' he said.

'Need any help, Dad?' asked Ross.

'It's OK. I'll ask Nkonko to come with me,' answered David, and he slipped outside into the light rain that was falling ahead of the storm.

For a while no one spoke inside the hut. Then Liz picked up Hannah's bowl of fruit and went over to the remaining chimps. 'Dinner time,' she announced, putting the dish inside the cage.

The sight of bananas and avocados seemed to rouse the babies out of their shocked lethargy. They snatched the food then pressed themselves against the back wall of the cage while they ate.

'Come on. Let's see if you want to go in with the others now,' Jake said, taking the injured male to the door of the cage. This time, the chimp didn't seem to mind at all. His attention fixed on the heap of fruit, he scampered inside and grabbed a banana.

'I think we should leave them alone now,' said Liz.

'Aren't we going to reunite them with Ashai?' Jake asked.

'Not yet. They need to rest first,' answered Liz. 'We'll see how they are in the morning.'

* * *

Jake was awake at first light the next day. He could hardly wait to see Ashai's reaction when she was reunited with members of her family. But he was also slightly anxious. Over dinner the night before, David had confirmed what Ross had said earlier. Only a few of the chimps were from the A-community – the injured male, the dead infant and one of the older females. The others must have been taken from another forest. And because they didn't belong to Ashai's community, she might react badly when she saw them.

After breakfast, Jake helped to take the six infants over to the holding pen. He carried the small male with the injured wrist while Ross took two of the other tiny ones across. Hannah and the Kirbys each carried a chimp too.

Jake thought the group of orphans seemed less traumatized today. They clung trustingly to their human foster parents while they looked round at the camp with wide, nervous eyes.

'I guess it's better if they're suspicious,' Jake observed to Ross as they approached the holding pen. 'They shouldn't really get too comfortable with humans.'

'No, never,' agreed Ross. 'Not unless all humans meant them no harm.'

'And that would be in a perfect world ...' murmured Liz.

In the holding pen, Ashai was sitting hunched up over a fresh termite mound. She stared into the nest, frowning intently.

David opened the gate and Ashai looked up, straight into Jake's eyes. '*Hoo?*' she hooted softly, as if asking a question.

'We've got a surprise for you,' Jake smiled, and at the same time, Ashai spotted the new chimps. She rose to her feet, her fur puffed out in consternation. '*Waa,*' she barked, her jaws opening slightly.

'It's your family,' Jake tried to explain as he followed David into the enclosure.

'OK,' said David when they were just inside the gate. 'Let's put them down and see what happens.'

The six orphans were staring wide-eyed at Ashai. They began to squeak and whimper, their jaws clenched and their teeth showing in nervous smiles.

'What if Ashai goes for them?' Jake asked, feeling the chimp on his hip grow tense. Now that he could compare Ashai directly with the others, he saw just how much bigger she was. She could probably do quite a lot of damage to the very tiny ones.

'It's a risk we'll have to take,' said Liz. 'And we're here to step in if necessary, although I'd rather they sorted themselves out.'

Jake set the little male down on the ground then watched closely as he began to shuffle towards Ashai, making soft panting hoots. Behind him, the others sat huddled together, looking confused and worried.

Ashai eyed the approaching chimp, then all of a sudden she let out a series of loud grunts that sounded just like laughter. With her mouth open in a wide grin, she scrambled over to the little male who ran straight towards her. The pair met in the middle of the pen and fell into each other's arms. Jake felt a dizzying surge of relief as they hugged and kissed each other, shrieking with excitement. It was obvious that Ashai and the little male recognized each other from their family group. Jake could only guess at Ashai's joy discovering that not all her family had been killed.

Next to Jake, Hannah was busy capturing the scene with her camera. 'This is too wonderful!' she murmured.

Then it was the turn of the others. The female that David had identified as also being from the A-community recognized Ashai just like the male had done. She went bounding over and gleefully joined in the noisy reunion, wrapping her arms tightly round Ashai's neck.

The remaining four followed more slowly, making

rapid soft panting sounds as if to show they meant no harm. Ashai sized them up with a wary gaze, her frown showing that she didn't recognize them. Jake braced himself, ready to sprint forward and scoop up the little ones if a fight broke out. '*Waa*,' Ashai coughed softly. The others paused and looked nervously at her. '*Hoo, hoo*,' they whimpered in response, their lips pushed forward in a pout.

Come on, Ashai, Jake urged silently. *Give them a break. They've had a hard time, too.*

The stand-off continued for a few more seconds until one of the babies started shuffling forward again. Grunting very faintly, he approached Ashai and stretched out one arm towards her. Ashai narrowed her eyes, then the expression on her face changed completely. She put her head on one side and, with a delighted grin, hooted at the little stranger.

Jake guessed this must have been some kind of invitation because the next moment, the little male was snuggling close to Ashai, even making clumsy attempts to groom her by plucking at her fur with his tiny fingers.

'Phew!' Jake breathed out quietly. 'For a minute I thought Ashai was going to send him packing.'

'So did I,' admitted Ross. 'I once saw a chimp about the same age as Ashai attack another young one really violently.'

'I'm glad you only told me that now,' Jake smiled as the last three chimps timidly approached Ashai. With one arm still wrapped around the little male, she reached out to welcome them, patting their heads and shoulders with heart-wrenching gentleness.

ELEVEN

'What happens next?' Jake asked when they were all standing outside the pen, watching the orphaned chimps from a distance.

'We'll give them time to get over their ordeal, then we'll find a new community for them to join,' answered David. 'Richard and Nkonko are going out today to track a particular group I have in mind.'

'Getting them into a new community sounds easy, but I bet it isn't,' observed Hannah.

'You said it!' David agreed. 'Introducing young chimps to each other is unpredictable enough. But with adults around, things can get out of hand pretty quickly.'

'You mean they might attack the babies?' Jake asked.

'I'm afraid that's quite likely,' said David. 'Chimps have a strong sense of group identity. They care a lot about members of their own community, but with outsiders they can be incredibly hostile.'

'Yeah, they'll brutally attack intruders – even kill them,' put in Ross.

'Kill them!' Jake echoed. He pushed away the picture that formed in his mind of angry adult chimps attacking the orphans. Instead, he concentrated on the infants feeding contentedly in the pen. Ashai finished her banana and loped away on all fours towards the termite nest. At once, the male with the injured wrist went scampering after her. When he caught her up, he scrambled on to her back, gripping with his toes and his good hand.

Jake waited for Ashai to shove him off, but she just carried on knuckling across the enclosure. 'How's that for hitch-hiking?' he chuckled.

'She's really doing the big sister thing,' agreed Ross.

'Can't we just let them become a community themselves?' Jake said. 'They could stay here until they're old enough to go into the forest on their own.'

'That would be ideal, except for one thing,' said Liz. 'Without adults, they'll never learn to fend for themselves. They'd have to be kept in captivity for the rest of their lives.' She smiled at Jake. 'With the best will in the world, we'd never be able to teach a chimp to be a chimp. We just don't have their skills.'

Jake grinned back at her. He guessed she was thinking of the failed termite-fishing lesson!

A loud whistle reached them from the far side of the camp. Jake looked across the clearing and saw Richard and Nkonko heading towards the forest. They carried large rucksacks on their backs and rifles slung over their shoulders. The scouts stopped and waved then went on.

'Let's hope they can find the XYZ-community,' said David.

'XYZ?' Jake frowned. 'Why do you call them that?'

'Because they're such a motley bunch,' grinned Ross. 'Not your average family of chimps.' More seriously, he added, 'The one thing they do have in common is that most of them have been through absolute hell.'

Liz nodded sombrely. 'Come to the lounge tent so we can show you some photographs and tell you all about them.'

As they walked away from the holding pen, Jake glanced over his shoulder at the chimpanzees. Ashai was sitting on her haunches, inspecting a nut. The male infant was leaning against her, one arm draped over her raised knees.

Jake saw Ashai pop the nut into her mouth. With her lips jutting out comically, she tried to crack open the shell with her teeth.

'I reckon she'll break her teeth before the nut,' said Ross, who had also stopped to watch.

'She needs a nutcracker,' Jake agreed.

At that moment, Ashai looked up and gazed directly at Jake. She grunted then spat out the nut crossly.

'Too hard for you, Ashai?' Jake called.

But Ashai wasn't giving up yet. Glancing round, she picked up a big stone and started to bash the nut with it.

'Another tool!' Jake said, surprised. 'A hammer.'

'That's right,' said Ross. 'Just like our Stone Age ancestors.'

Despite Ashai's best efforts, the nut would not break open. Frustrated, Ashai raised the stone above her head then brought it down with a loud thud. But the impact just made the nut go shooting across the ground.

Jake couldn't help laughing. 'Better luck next time, Ashai!'

The chimp hunched her shoulders and blinked at him, pouting miserably. Jake realized that Ashai's clumsy attempts to crack the nut made it clear that she still needed lots of guidance in forest survival from adult chimps. The best option had to be for her to join a new community. But would they accept her?

'Let's go and see the photos of her new family,' Jake said to Ross, turning towards the tents.

Inside the lounge tent, Liz was opening a big wooden box. 'We have to keep everything under lock and key here,' she said.

'Do you really get thieves out here?' asked Hannah.

'You bet,' grinned Ross. 'Baboons, chimps, monkeys! They'll have a go at anything we leave lying around. Last week, one came in and shredded a whole wad of chemistry notes I'd left on the table.'

'You're joking!' Jake exclaimed.

'No,' said Ross, pulling a face. 'It meant I had to start all over again.'

Liz took out a shoe box marked *XYZ Community*. 'We never seem to have time to put our photos in albums,' she said apologetically, taking off the lid.

The box was packed with photographs of chimps, their wise wrinkled faces looking benignly out at Jake. But as Liz began passing the pictures around, Jake realized that these were no ordinary chimpanzees. Nearly all of them had some kind of scar or injury. A couple were even missing limbs.

'I see what you meant about them going through hell,' Jake said to Ross. He stared at a picture of a young chimp with a rope tied round its waist. 'What happened to this one?'

'That's Mtoto,' replied Ross. 'Remember I told you about the one that bonded with me a few years ago?'

Jake nodded.

Ross continued. 'Well, a woman tried to smuggle her across the border on her back, like a human baby. But the police spotted her and confiscated Mtoto. We took that picture the day she arrived here. The poachers had tied her up to stop her escaping and the rope was so tight it left scars on her hips.'

'That's cruel!' Jake burst out. 'And stupid. What did they think the chimp would do?' He thought about the seven orphans in the pen. None of them had ever looked as if they would try to run away. They were all too confused and frightened.

'There's a lot people don't realize about chimpanzees,' said Liz. 'Look at this, for example.' She handed Jake another photograph.

The picture showed a young male chimp sitting behind bars. A man in a white coat was standing in front of the cage. He had a syringe in one hand and a medicine phial in the other. But what made Jake's blood run cold was the row of numbers on the chimp's chest.

'Laboratory numbers,' David explained quietly before Jake could ask the question. 'His chest was shaved and the numbers tattooed on.'

Jake felt sick with horror. 'You mean this chimp was used for experiments?'

'Uh-huh,' said David.

'How did you rescue this one?' asked Hannah.

'An animal rights organization managed to have the laboratory closed down,' said Liz. 'Most of the chimps were in such a bad way they had to be destroyed, but three were fit enough to be shipped out to us.' She sorted through the photographs and found one showing the newly arrived chimpanzees.

The laboratory chimps stared out from the picture with blank eyes. Their heads drooped between their hunched-up shoulders and their coats looked thin and ragged.

'How long did it take for them to recover?' asked Hannah.

'A couple of years,' said Liz. 'At first we thought they'd have to remain in captivity, but they surprised us with their resilience. And when we introduced them to a pair of adult sisters who'd been trapped in a snare, they went from strength to strength.'

'That's when we thought about releasing the five of them into the forest together,' said David. 'Later, others like Mtoto joined them. Somehow, chimps that have been rescued from desperate circumstances are more tolerant of outsiders than ordinary wild chimps.'

'So that's why you want Ashai and the others to join this group,' Jake said. He picked up a photograph showing a large group of chimps lazing about in a shady clearing. He recognized several of the individuals from other photos. 'Is this the whole XYZ-community?' he asked.

'Pretty much,' said Ross. 'There are about ten in the group now.'

'And a couple of their own babies too,' smiled Liz. 'Which just shows how well the group has adapted to its new life.'

'I'd love to see those babies,' said Hannah, her eyes shining.

'With any luck you will,' David told her. 'Once Richard and Nkonko find out where the community is.'

The scouts returned late the next afternoon to report that they had located the XYZ-community in a remote part of the forest sanctuary. Jake was very relieved when David told them the area was regularly patrolled by armed guards. If the seven orphans were accepted into the community, they'd be as safe as they could be from more attacks. The Kumalo brothers may have been caught, but Jake was realistic enough to know that others would come in their place.

'We'll leave first thing in the morning,' said David over dinner.

All night, Jake tossed and turned, thinking about everything that could go wrong with the release of the orphans. The XYZ-group might reject them completely or, worse still, the infants might cling to their human rescuers and refuse to join the other chimps. And then there were the tiniest babies. Was it safe to leave them with a bunch of strangers in the forest?

By morning, Jake had convinced himself that the operation was doomed to failure. Feeling groggy and worried, he dressed quickly and joined the others in the boma for breakfast.

'It's going to be a tough hike,' David warned as they tucked into steaming maize porridge. 'The community is about four hours from here and it's uphill most of the way.'

'That's OK,' said Ross. 'It means it'll be downhill all the way back!'

Because everyone from the camp was going on the hike, they locked everything away and zipped up the tents. Then they went to fetch the orphans.

Jake's gloomy mood lifted the moment he saw the babies. For the first time since they'd been rescued, the chimps were playing. Ashai was tickling one of the smaller babies, while two others were tumbling about on the ground, hooting their soft chimp laugh.

'They look great!' Jake laughed. He watched one of the smallest babies reaching up to grab the legs of another that was dangling from a branch. 'You'd never think they'd had such a bad time the other day.'

'Just goes to show how much spirit they have,' said Hannah.

When David opened the gate, the chimps stopped playing and glanced across curiously at him. They'd had little contact with the humans since they'd arrived at Luama. This was to make sure they bonded with each other instead.

'Guess what?' Jake said, going in and crossing over to Ashai. The chimp stared at him, her bottom lip protruding in a pout. 'You're going back into the forest,' Jake told her, stretching out one hand. 'Come on. You can hold my hand like you did the other day.' He waited for her to respond, but she sat silently, frowning at him.

Jake drew his hand back. He wondered what was going through Ashai's mind. Did she have some way of knowing that she was about to leave the pen for good? *For good!* The words echoed in Jake's head, as if to remind him that after today, he might never see Ashai again. His mind flashed back to when he'd first heard her whimpering in the forest. He felt so privileged that she'd chosen to trust him after other humans had treated her so cruelly. He reached out his hand to her again. 'Hoo, hoo, hoo,' he breathed, wanting somehow to tell her he'd never forget her.

Ashai's expression softened and she blinked slowly at him. *Hoo, hoo, waa*, she panted. Then she reached out and brushed the tips of his fingers before pulling her hand away.

Jake chuckled. 'OK, you don't have to hold my hand. Are you feeling all grown-up now that you're the oldest?'

Ashai copied Jake's chuckle but stopped abruptly when she saw the rest of her group being taken out of the pen. When Ross scooped up the tiny male with the injured wrist, she charged angrily over to him. With a threatening shout, she pulled at the baby's arm.

'It's OK,' Ross tried to convince Ashai. 'I'm not hurting him.'

But Ashai wouldn't give in. Eventually Ross had to hand the baby to her. With a satisfied grunt, Ashai hoisted the infant on to her back.

'Sure, you can carry him if you want,' shrugged Ross.

Pouting with determination, Ashai stayed where she was and watched him go out of the pen.

'Come on,' said Jake. 'Let's go.' He went over to the gate but Ashai didn't follow him. Jake looked back at her. She was glancing around the empty pen with a puzzled expression.

Jake beckoned to her. 'It's time to go,' he said.

Ashai slapped herself across her chest and whimpered then, with the tiny male still clinging to her back, she dropped on to all fours and ran across to Jake. It looked like she was ready to leave her temporary home.

TWELVE

'What if we can't find the XYZ-group?' Jake asked Ross, his earlier anxiety returning. They were toiling up a steep, thickly wooded slope that seemed to go on for ever. It was hot and uncomfortably humid. Not even a whisper of wind disturbed the leaves, and apart from the laboured breathing of the humans and their soft footfalls, the only sound was the shrill chorus of cicadas in the trees.

Next to Jake, Ashai loped along easily with the wounded male still riding on her back. The other remaining female from the A-community plodded along just behind her. Like a little sister, she had tailed Ashai all the way through the forest. Next, came the other larger infant. He had refused to let anyone carry him, so Jake was keeping a watchful eye on him to make sure he didn't get left behind.

'Oh, we'll find the community all right,' answered Ross, craning his neck to look over the head of the infant in his arms. 'Nkonko said they were feeding at a clump of oil-nut palms. If there's plenty to eat, they'll probably hang around there for a few days.'

At the top of the hill, they stopped to rest. Jake sat down on a tree trunk and took out his water flask. Ashai shoved the jockey-chimp off her back and pulled herself on to the mossy log next to Jake. She stared as he took a swig of water then hesitantly poked at the flask with one finger.

'Want some?' Jake offered it to her.

Ashai grinned widely, showing her pink gums, and took the flask from Jake. She stuck a finger into the opening then pulled it out and sucked it.

'That's not how you do it,' Jake chuckled. He tried to take the flask back from Ashai but she leaned away from him, clinging to it. 'And it's not yours, anyway,' he added.

Ashai glared at him. '*Waa*,' she barked as if telling Jake to back off, then, with a low grunt, she upended the flask above her mouth. The water gushed out, drenching her face and soaking into her furry neck.

'Nope, you don't do it like that either,' Jake told her with a smile.

Ashai blinked and wiped a hand across her wet face. She peered into the flask then fastened her lips around the top of it and made exaggerated sucking noises. Realizing it was empty, she took it out of her mouth and banged it against the log a few times. Finally, she tossed it casually to the ground.

'Thanks very much!' Jake said, picking it up and putting it on the log next to him. 'Didn't anyone ever tell you about not dropping litter?'

'It comes naturally to them,' laughed Ross, who had been watching. 'You can always tell where chimps have been. They leave behind piles of fruit skins, ant-fishing sticks, bits of bark, broken branches – you name it.'

Liz wrestled a bunch of bananas out of her rucksack. The tiny chimp clinging to her side started squealing with excitement. The rest of the orphans spun round to see what the fuss was about and within seconds, Liz was surrounded by them all. 'Cupboard love!' she joked. 'I just hope this is the last time you get a free meal from us.'

David and Richard were looking through their binoculars at a ridge on the other side of the densely forested valley.

'Is it much further?' asked Hannah.

'Not far now,' Nkonko promised her. He shifted his rifle from one shoulder to the other and pointed to the ridge. 'The community was in that area yesterday.'

'And I think they're still there,' said David. 'I'm pretty sure I can see a couple of them up a palm tree.'

'Brilliant,' Jake said. He jumped up, knocking the flask off the log. Before he could pick it up, Ashai scampered over and grabbed it. With a disapproving frown, she held it up to Jake and grunted softly.

'Sorry!' Jake laughed. 'I didn't mean to litter your forest.'

Heavy black clouds were gathering by the time the party reached the ridge. A distant rumbling in the atmosphere warned of an impending storm. Even the cicadas grew quiet as if they couldn't compete with the sound of thunder.

'Oh, great!' Jake muttered, feeling big drops of rain splatter against his face and arms. 'Now we'll never find the chimps.' He was sure the storm would send them into hiding.

'Don't worry,' said Ross, as if he could guess what Jake was thinking. 'Chimps don't usually shelter from the rain. They just sit out in the open all hunched up, waiting for it to stop.'

'And that's where the difference in DNA comes in,' chuckled Hannah, stopping to take out her anorak. 'I'm certainly not going to get drenched if I can help it!'

They all paused to pull on their rain gear then trudged on through the dripping forest. Half an hour further on, Richard stopped and put his fingers to his lips. 'Listen,' he whispered.

Jake held his breath. Above the patter of the raindrops, he could just make out the familiar sound of a chimpanzee hooting in the distance. Next to him, Ashai heard it too. She froze and stared in the direction the hooting was coming from, then she slipped her hand into Jake's and whimpered anxiously.

Jake squeezed her hand, trying to reassure her. It felt like he was taking a child to her first day at school. He looked at the six other chimps. They were also peering ahead, looking tense and nervous.

Richard beckoned to everyone to move on. In silence, they approached some towering palm trees. Suddenly, Nkonko motioned to them to stop. 'Over there,' he mouthed, pointing.

Just beyond the trees, three adult chimpanzees sat huddled together in a clearing, their shoulders hunched up and their arms around their knees. With a jolt, Jake realized that one of them had only one arm, and he remembered the limbless chimps in the photos. He pointed the chimp out to Ross who nodded and whispered, 'Caught in a snare.'

David crouched down on the ground and studied the small group through his binoculars. 'All females,' he whispered. He watched them for a few minutes then stood up. 'We'll put the little ones nearby and see what happens.'

Because the XYZ-group was used to seeing the scouts, Richard and Nkonko each carried two of the infants to within several metres of the three adults. They put the babies on the ground then backed away slowly.

Jake tried to encourage Ashai to go forward by pointing to the other babies and giving her a gentle nudge. But Ashai dug in her heels and refused to budge. Her two younger companions stood next to her, clinging to her arms.

Liz signalled to Jake. 'It's OK,' she mouthed. 'David will take them later.'

Jake watched the four babies sitting forlornly on the wet ground. The XYZ females seemed to be ignoring them. They sat motionless with their heads drooping, staring into the rain.

'They're just not interested in the babies,' whispered Hannah, kneeling down next to Jake with her camera at the ready.

The infants grew restless and started to whimper, bunching together closely. One of the adults glanced across at them. She shook her head and drops of water scattered around her, then she fell back into her melancholy stare.

Jake felt frustrated. He'd imagined all sorts of reactions to the orphans, but never complete indifference.

A loud rumble sounded through the forest. Jake thought it was thunder. The noise came again, and this time, all the chimpanzees reacted. A shiver of excitement ran through them. Even Ashai tightened her grip on Jake's hand, while in the middle of the clearing the tiny infants looked around with wide frightened eyes.

Suddenly, an enormous male chimpanzee appeared in a tree on the far side of the clearing. With a deafening *wraaa* he swung down to the ground and picked up a broken bough. He glared at the huddle of females and swaggered towards them on his hind legs, hooting loudly and brandishing the branch.

'Now what?' Jake breathed to Ross.

'That's Mjeuri,' whispered Ross. 'Showing off as usual.'

Mjeuri shook the branch above the females, sprinkling them with leaves and raindrops, but they ignored him. He gave another loud hoot then sat down, popped a palm nut into his mouth and cracked the shell in his strong yellow teeth. He spat out the hard casing and chewed the soft kernel, glancing round the clearing.

Suddenly he noticed the babies. He barked and stood up, his fur bristling and his brown eyes narrowed. Then he dropped on to all fours and scooted over to the orphans. Jake dug his fingernails into his palms, fighting the urge to run to the tiny chimps and grab them out of Mjeuri's way. Mjeuri loomed over the four infants, barking crossly.

This is a mistake, Jake thought. The infants were in terrible danger. Perhaps Mjeuri even meant to kill them! He shot a look at David and the scouts, half-expecting them to shoot into the air to frighten Mjeuri away. But the men stood with their arms folded and their rifles hanging down at their sides.

How can they be so calm? Jake wondered. He looked back at the chimps. The four babies crouched in front of the angry male, squeaking and grunting in fear. One of them even turned his back in submission then, grinning nervously, peered at Mjeuri over his shoulder.

This did nothing to calm Mjeuri. With an angry *wraaa*, he grabbed the baby's arm and swung him into the air.

'No!' Jake burst out, scrambling to his feet.

But Nkonko caught his hand and stopped him. 'He'll go for you too,' he whispered.

The tiny chimp was dangling upside down from Mjeuri's huge hand, screaming in sheer terror. Jake could hardly bare to look. 'It's as bad as being caught by poachers,' he protested quietly, biting his lip. He threw David an appealing look. 'Please help them,' he begged.

'I can't,' David said. 'He'd get even angrier.'

A fork of lightning shot across the sky, cracking the air like a whip. This seemed to enrage Mjeuri even more. He pressed his lips together and shook the baby roughly.

Suddenly one of the adult females stood up and ran over to Mjeuri. The huge male hooted and dropped the baby to the ground. The female scooped up the screaming baby and cuddled him close to her while giving Mjeuri a withering look. The tough adult male knitted his brows together then, pouting sulkily, turned and plodded away into the forest. As soon as he'd gone, the other two females loped across and began fussing over the frightened babies.

'About time too,' Jake breathed, feeling his heart rate return to normal.

Beside him, there was an audible sigh of relief as everyone watched the adult chimpanzees patting and soothing the little ones. Mjeuri's hostility seemed to have provoked them into showing maternal interest in the new arrivals. And when the females finally turned and headed back across the clearing with the babies clinging to their chests, or riding like jockeys on their backs, David turned to give the others a cautious thumbs-up.

'It's looking good,' he whispered. 'But we'll keep an eye on them for the next few weeks, just to make sure the babies are fully accepted into the group.'

'Look, here come the others,' said Liz, pointing to the other side of the clearing where several other chimpanzees had silently appeared. They waited for the three females to join them before inspecting the newcomers with gentle curiosity.

'There's another baby,' Jake remarked, seeing a tiny black infant clinging to its mother.

'Hey! I think the mother is Mtoto,' said Ross, his eyes lighting up. He turned to David. 'She's had a baby. Isn't that brilliant?'

'You can say that again,' said his dad. 'Nkonko and Richard didn't see her yesterday, so we were a bit worried about her.'

Jake felt Ashai's hand slip out of his. 'Well, little one?' he said to her. 'Are you going to join the others?'

Ashai grunted quietly and took a few uneven steps into the clearing. The last two orphans scuttled after her. *Hoo, hoo, waa*, Ashai panted, padding slowly forward again.

On the other side of the clearing, the XYZ-group looked up, their hair bristling in alarm.

Hoo, hoo, waa, repeated Ashai, moving cautiously towards them. The little male whimpered anxiously at her side and she paused long enough to let him climb on to her back.

Beads of sweat broke out on Jake's forehead. Ashai was older than the other infants. Too old for the XYZ-females to want to adopt her like the babies?

Halfway across the clearing, Ashai paused again. She sat down, shooting a timid glance at the large group opposite her. She blinked and looked away, then started to groom the two infants with her.

One of the adult females stood up and came forward. It was Mtoto. She held her own baby protectively in one arm as she ambled over to Ashai's little group.

Hoo, hoo, hoo, panted Ashai nervously.

Mtoto sat down a few metres from Ashai and stared at her. Mtoto's infant peered round over his shoulder, his tiny pink face wrinkled with curiosity. Seeing the newcomers, he slid to the ground and tottered unsteadily towards them.

'Watch out, Ashai!' Jake whispered. 'This could mean trouble.' But Mtoto just watched her baby as he stopped to pick up a palm nut.

Mtoto's child studied the nut as if he was trying to work out how to eat it. He dropped it on the ground and stamped on it clumsily with one tiny foot. The nut rolled away from him. He scampered after it but before he could pick it up, Ashai leaned over and grabbed it.

'Don't!' Jake winced.

The baby whimpered and reached for the nut but Ashai turned away. Mtoto stiffened and puffed out her fur.

'Here we go,' Jake heard Ross whisper under his breath. He braced himself for another terrifying confrontation.

With her head tipped thoughtfully on one side, Ashai dropped the nut on the ground. Then she curled her fingers round a big stone and slammed it down on the nut. The shell split open and Ashai picked out the kernel. Instead of gobbling it down herself, she handed it to Mtoto's infant. The baby pushed the kernel into his mouth and curled his top lip with pleasure.

'Well, would you look at that!' Jake breathed.

Beside him, his mum's camera clicked frantically. 'Ashai's a natural mother,' Hannah smiled, lowering her camera. 'And it's this sort of picture that might persuade people in other parts of the world to join the battle against poaching.'

'It sounds like you've decided to change the focus of your magazine article,' said Liz.

'Absolutely,' replied Hannah. 'After everything I've seen here, I want to do more than just report on cute chimp behaviour. I'm thinking of doing a series of articles that will show just how bad the situation is for African primates.' She lifted her camera again.

The shutter clicked just as Mtoto shuffled forward to pick up her baby.

The adult female reached out a long shaggy arm and patted Ashai and her two little companions on their heads. Ashai's troubled face relaxed and broke into a wide, toothy grin.

'That's clinched it for sure,' grinned Ross.

'Yep!' said David. 'Fingers crossed, the XYZ-community is now seven chimps stronger.'

Mtoto stood up. She glanced round, almost as if she knew she had an audience, then ambled back to the rest of her group.

Ashai and the two other orphans didn't hesitate. Looking like they'd always been a part of Mtoto's group, they scampered after her.

Just short of the adult group, Ashai skidded to a halt. She turned and looked back, as if she'd forgotten something. *Hoo, hoo, hoo,* she whimpered plaintively. The hairs stood up on the back of Jake's neck. Ashai's call was achingly familiar to him now.

But this time, Jake didn't hoot back. *You don't need me any more, Ashai*, he urged her silently. *This is your home now.*

Ashai hooted again, her voice rising questioningly. She waited, her eyes fixed on the trees where Jake was standing. He stood very still, biting his lip and fighting back the urge to reply.

Finally, Ashai seemed to accept there would be no answer. Shaking her head, she pushed her lips forward in a pout, then dropped on to all fours and followed her new family into the forest.

This series is dedicated to Virginia McKenna and Bill Travers, founders of the Born Free Foundation, and to George and Joy Adamson, who inspired them and so many others to love and respect wild animals. If you would like to find out more about the work of the Born Free Foundation, please visit their website, www.bornfree.org.uk, or call 01403 240170.